THE REAL QUESTION

Published by
PEACHTREE PUBLISHERS
1700 Chattahoochee Avenue
Atlanta, Georgia 30318-2112
www.peachtree-online.com

Text © 2006 by Adrian Fogelin

First trade paperback edition published in 2009

Book and cover design by Loraine M. Joyner
Composition by Melanie McMahon Ives

Cover photograph © 2006 by Luke Winn

Printed in the United States of America
10 9 8 7 6 5 4 3 2 1 (hardcover)
10 9 8 7 6 5 4 3 2 1 (trade paperback)

Library of Congress Cataloging-in-Publication Data

Fogelin, Adrian.
  The real question / by Adrian Fogelin. -- 1st ed.
     p. cm.
  Summary: Fisher Brown, a sixteen-year-old over-achiever, is on the verge of academic burnout when he impulsively decides to stop cramming for the SATs for one
weekend and accompany his ne'er-do-well neighbor to an out-of-town job repairing
a roof.
  ISBN 13: 978-1-56145-383-2 / ISBN 10: 1-56145-383-8 (hardcover)
  ISBN 13: 978-1-56145-501-0 / ISBN 10: 1-56145-501-6 (trade paperback)
  [1. Coming of age--Fiction. 2. Single-parent families--Fiction. 3. Schools--Fiction.
4. Fathers and sons--Fiction. 5. Interpersonal relations--Fiction. 6. Florida--Fiction.]
I. Title.

PZ7.F72635Re 2006
[Fic]--dc22

                                                        2006013996

THE
REAL
QUESTION

ADRIAN FOGELIN
Author of THE BIG NOTHING

*This one's for the kids I shared the back seat with:
my sister Claudia and my brother Carl Christian.
Are we there yet?*

Thanks to my dear friends,
the Wednesday Night Writers:
Richard Dempsey, Gina Edwards,
Leigh Muller, and Noanne Gwynn.

Thanks to Vicky Holifield, extraordinary editor,
keeper of both the forest and the trees.

And heartfelt thanks to two people who made
Fisher and the world of high school overachieving real:
overachiever Taylor Wolff (as a straight-B student
I could never have imagined Fisher without your help)
and Margo Hall, former principal of Leon High School—
your generosity with your knowledge of high school students
is exceeded only by your affection for them.

1

ne second ago the brain was multitasking up a storm—
processing questions, accessing formulas, monitoring
the clock—not to mention calculating my chances of
beating out the usual competition, Hofstra and Raleigh.

The brain put away the easy questions first, standard procedure when test questions are equally weighted.

After a quick scan it passed on number three: old material. Leave it to Millikan to pull something from a couple of
units back. Plus, it looked complex—not killer, but time con-
suming—lots of conversions.

Now I've finished the others and I'm back, staring at
number three, my fist choking the pencil: *A sample of dry gas
weighing 2.1025 g is found to occupy 2.850 L at 82.0 degrees
Fahrenheit and 740.0 mm Hg. How many moles of the gas are present?* Time to dust off the old ideal gas law: $PV = nRT$. Millikan calls it "pivnert." But when I get to the conversions,
I've got nothing. The value for R? The conversion to
Kelvin? The brain can't shake the information loose. All I

have is Millikan's stupid "pivnert." Pivnert… pivnert…the brain sputters. It's like facing the blue screen of death when your CPU dies—a complete brain crash.

I back up, read the problem again, but this time the words fail to register; is this thing even written in English?

I cross-check the one above it, the one below, problems I burned through minutes ago. Suddenly, they don't make sense either. What the hell is happening?

I knew all this crap last night. I knew it at five this morning. All those hours chained to my desk? I *know* this stuff. Why can't I access it?

Pencils scratch paper—no one else is having a problem. While the doom clock over Millikan's desk obliterates the final minutes, I wipe my sweaty palms on my jeans and try to breathe; all of a sudden it's hard.

God, I'm having a stroke!

Can a person have a stroke at sixteen?

I don't think so, not unless they're shooting hoops and have a bad heart valve or something.

Maybe I'm the first: Honors Student Strokes Out in Chemistry Exam.

Concentrate. Got to concentrate. As I stare at the question, my field of vision shrinks. Words break down to letters. I'm seeping through the spaces between them.

Hofstra shifts in the chair behind mine. His pencil hits the desk. He's done. One through twenty-five, inclusive—done.

From further down the row I hear a chair creak. Crap! Raleigh's done too.

Thirty seconds left. But now the letters are disintegrating, becoming quivering molecules of ink on paper. The pencil slips in my sweaty hand.

"Time," barks Millikan. "Pass your exams forward."

Hofstra flaps a stack of papers against my back. I take the tests, add mine, and pass them up; the stack moves along like some small hapless mammal being ingested by a snake.

We've got three minutes to kill before the bell. Millikan has no mercy. He could have given us those three minutes. It might have come back to me.

But when I close my eyes I see those ink molecules uncoupling, devolving into their constituent atoms. I'm scaring the shit out of myself.

All around the room the complaining begins. "Man, that sucked!" "Yeah, big time."

"How'd you guys do?" Raleigh's voice. The test isn't cold yet and Raleigh's checking the competition. "Fisher?"

"I tanked on number three."

"One wrong is still a 96. How about the other twenty-four?"

"Think I did okay." Under my desk I press two fingers against my wrist. I usually have to run miles to make my pulse surge like this.

"Hofstra?" Raleigh asks.

Behind me I hear a dull thud. "I am so dead," Hofstra groans.

When I turn, his forehead is on the desk, the top vertebra in his neck sticking up.

Raleigh detects blood in the water. "Number three elude you too?" He hops up and squats on his chair.

"Three…four…five…" Hofstra slams his head repeatedly, ramming the desk forward with each head bang. "Basically, all of them."

"No lie! *All?*" Even Raleigh's frizzy hair seems to perk up. "Define *all.*"

"One through twenty-five. All. I totally zoned."

"Twenty-five percent of the final grade!" Raleigh crows.

"Quit gloating," I say quietly, watching him grin like a malevolent elf.

"Who's gloating?" he asks, still wearing his triumph like a Hawaiian shirt. "Okay, okay. I am. But think about it. A slide by Hofstra could affect the world order. I could move up. You could move up."

Hofstra mumbles something into the desktop.

"Quit talking to the desk," advises Raleigh.

Hofstra rotates his neck just enough so his forehead is no longer in contact with wood. "Consider the Just Man." Leave it to Hofstra to bring in one of the Great Dead Ones. "According to Socrates, the Just Man wants only to best the Unjust Man," he explains to Raleigh, who, perhaps wisely, has steered clear of Classics. "The Unjust Man wants to beat the crap out of everybody."

Raleigh shrugs. "There's a little bit of the Unjust Man in all of us, right, Fisher?"

Under cover of the ringing bell I ask, "Are you okay, Hofstra?" Unlike Raleigh, who is 95 percent petty annoyance, Hofstra's a friend.

"I'm fine." He throws his big, bony hands open. "It's no big deal, okay?"

4

"Only life or death," Raleigh points out as he follows us into the hall. "Among the three of us we have next year's valedictorian, salutatorian, and one guy who's going to wish he'd tried just a little harder. That lucky guy could be you, Hofstra—there goes your shot at becoming a nuclear physicist."

Hands in his pockets, shoulders hunched, Hofstra looks even skinnier and more bent than usual. "Think I'll become pope instead."

"You're not even Catholic," I point out.

He shrugs. "I could join. It would be fun to be infallible. We're not having fun now, that's for sure."

"Fun comes later." Raleigh jumps in front of Hofstra. Walking backwards down the hall, he cramps Hofstra's long, gangly strides. "You forget. We're working on the Deferred Gratification Model. The payoff is down the road when one of us walks into our twentieth reunion as the next Bill Gates."

"My money's on Hofstra," I say.

"Why him?" asks Raleigh.

"Come on. My brain is decent; yours is too. Hofstra's is scary."

"We keep up," he protests, getting trapped behind an open locker door.

"Only because we outwork him," I call back. Hofstra and I, both really tall, scout the thin spots in the herd. Raleigh disappears behind us as we move through the crowd. "So, what was your problem in there?" I ask. There's a chance we both got infected by some airborne pathogen—like Legionnaires' disease—only this one affects brain function.

"No sleep," he mumbles. Red creeps up his neck and across the acne battlefield of his face. "I met this girl online last night. A warrior babe named Xandra."

"You sure it's a girl?" Raleigh asks, suddenly reappearing between the shoulders of two Leon High T-shirts. "Online, Xandra could be anybody…a guy, a dwarf, a nun—"

Hofstra whips around. "No, she's for real."

"As in corporeal, actual, verifiable, authentic?" Raleigh's got to be studying for the SAT Verbals—the guy never makes a bad academic move.

But neither do I. It's Hofstra who coasts. Smart as he is, he sublimates tests, gets lost in cyberspace, binge-drinks. He sabotages himself. I work my ass off.

So why was I the one who had total brain lock?

I bounce the point of my pencil on the library table. It's four-twenty and Annie's late. As usual. In her universe she's blowing off algebra. In mine she's standing me up.

Hofstra goes online to get girls (or dwarfs, or nuns); I get them with a business card printed on my Epson:

Geek for Hire.
Fisher Brown can teach math to your hamster.
(A passing grade guaranteed or your money back.)
555-5175

All I learned when Annie Cagney called for tutoring was that she was a sophomore repeating Algebra IB. I didn't realize I was talking to the mystery blonde from the hall until she walked into the library for our first session. *Yes!* I thought. *There is a god!*

Before that I'd only seen her between second and third and at school events like last Saturday's choir concert. Dez—my friend Desiree—invited me. I went because I knew Annie the Beautiful would be standing on the riser below her. One voice soared over the others. It made the skin on my arms tingle. The voice belonged to Dez, but I was watching only Annie. I gave the voice to her. The other singers disappeared. Annie, all by herself, sang in Dez's beautiful voice as she glowed and kind of floated in her blue choir robe. Then, since this was my fantasy, I pictured her in something more MTV—I tried out various outfits.

Okay, it's lame. But I don't have much to work with. Our only one-on-one is actually a threesome: her, me, and algebra. I haven't made much progress on the romantic front. In fact, I haven't made much progress with her on any front. Her brain is a string of Christmas lights with an intermittent short. She seems to grasp a concept, but by the next time we meet—*blink*—it's gone. If she were anyone else I'd give up and say bring on the hamster, but I can't.

I need to be around Annie.

To graduate, Annie needs to pass Algebra IB.

Why am I here and she isn't?

Guess I need to be around her more than she needs to pass Algebra IB.

I resort to doing Latin homework.

"Hey," says a small, breathy voice. I look up and there she is. My heart races, but I try to keep my tone indifferent. "Not to state the obvious, but you're fifty minutes late."

She swoons into the chair next to mine and falls against me, crying.

"Hey, it's…it's okay," I stutter. "What's a few minutes? Ask anyone, my time is worthless."

She snatches handfuls of my sweater and twists.

"Whoa, Annie, what's going on?" This is like a good dream gone bad.

Between sobs she explains she just had a blowout fight with her boyfriend.

Boyfriend? Of course a girl like her would have one. But between second and third when our paths cross in the hall, there's never a guy with her. Girlfriends, yes, but never a guy.

"Why is he like that?" she sobs. "All I said was, 'Ramos, how come you didn't call me last night?'"

"Ramos…Ramos Cruz, the quarterback?"

She nods against my chest, her hair tickling my neck. "I didn't know you liked football," she sniffs.

Actually, she doesn't know anything about me, but she's making physical contact so I let it slide. "Ramos and I used to be tight."

"*You* and Ramos?" Crying her eyes out, she still manages to sound skeptical.

I shift subtly and her cheek is pressed against my sweater. "Best friends, as a matter of fact." I don't mention it only lasted a semester, and it was sixth grade. I have to admit, the fact that we were ever friends is staggering, even to me.

But at the time we seemed the same. Or maybe it was just that we were undifferentiated, like cells that hadn't yet specialized. When we did differentiate, I specialized in acing every class. Ramos specialized in throwing long.

Dez says I miss the important stuff while obsessing about the insignificant. Annie the Beautiful is pressed against me and what am I doing? Reliving sixth grade.

I close my eyes and fold my arms around her. Wow. It's like she hit the perfume counter and sampled everything.

If I smell her, does she smell me? Did I put on deodorant this morning? Of course, I did. It's part of the routine.

But is it still working? That's the critical question. I resist the urge to sniff a pit.

"Should I apologize to him?" she moans.

"No," I say. "Definitely not." My shoulder feels wet. Her tears have soaked through to my shirt. I hold her carefully, afraid she'll realize the algebra guy's arms are around her.

With a shuddery sigh she presses herself into my chest, and at that exact moment, through the thin fabric of her blouse, my fingers detect the fastener of her bra.

I stumble off the late bus. With only one degree of separation I touched Annie's bra—in fact, the part of the bra that facilitates removal. Hofstra would give major points. Too bad it was meaningless. Ten seconds later, while I sat staring at the book open to the quadratic formula, she was whimpering into her cell, "Please, Ramos, please?"

FYI: Ramos Cruz is number one on her speed dial. What are the odds that the Geek-for-Hire is even on the list?

I kick a rock and jog up the hill, fishing the key out of my pocket as I go. I let myself into the empty house. Taking the stairs three at a time, I sprint to my room. I change into my Nikes. As I toss my sweater over the back of my desk chair, I discover the latest index card taped to the windowsill: *What is the real question?* Sounds cosmic, but since it was put there by my guidance counselor dad, it's bound to be test related. He's advising me to identify the intent of the question before answering—or something like that. This card joins all the other subtle hints taped up around my room.

I've never caught him in the act. Dad is the tooth fairy of test preparation.

I throw on a sweatshirt and just happen to look out the window as a guy saunters out of the house across the street. The last few days, whenever I'm at my desk studying, he's been out there loitering at the end of Mr. Traynor's driveway. He's wearing the same frayed jeans, the same cowboy boots he has worn every other day. I assume he changes the shirt, but clean or dirty, a white T-shirt is always part of the outfit. Doesn't he have anywhere to go, anything to do?

When the guy reaches the end of the driveway, he squats on his heels, face turned up to the sun. Eyes closed, he reaches back and casually peels off his T-shirt.

Come on. Winters aren't that cold in Tallahassee, but today's not exactly sunbathing weather. Besides, the sun is going down.

He wads up the T-shirt for a pillow and stretches out on

the strip of grass at the edge of the road, oblivious to what the local dogs use that grass for.

What is the real question? The index card on the windowsill suddenly seems like a caption for the scene outside. When it comes to identifying the real question I don't have a clue, but it's obvious that this guy and I are coming up with different answers.

All work and no play.

All play and no work.

Before starting to run I stand at the end of my driveway and watch the stranger in Mr. Traynor's yard. As his muscular chest rises and falls in deep, even breaths, a repulsive image pops into my brain. What would happen if he met Annie? Abort. Abort. I shut the simulation down. Isn't one muscular guy in her life enough?

Besides, the chances that they'll meet are infinitesimal. Like almost everything else, his presence across the street from my house at this precise moment can be explained by the math term Random Walk: a sequence of movements in which the direction of each successive movement is determined entirely at random.

I think about my own sequence of movements. What would have happened if I'd randomly walked a path more like Ramos's? I push up my sweatshirt sleeves and check out my spindly arms. Too late for that.

I take off running, flat out. As the houses flash by I feel looser, saner.

I started running because Dad insisted that to be a "complete package" I needed a sport. At one-sixty I'm too light for football. At six-foot-five you'd think I'd be a natural for basketball. Too bad I'm a complete spaz. Dad's friend, Coach Dickerson, suggested track, but I didn't make the cut. I expend more energy on vertical motion than horizontal when I run.

Last year I went out for cross-country—they take anyone who's still standing at the end of the distance. Cross-country is over for the year, but I keep running for the endorphin rush.

Me and my endorphin buddies tour the neighborhood. My eyeglasses bounce on the bridge of my nose, beating the same rhythm as my feet, only a nanosecond behind. I pass the sleeping guy twice.

I'm rounding the corner by my house for a third time when the guy yelps, "Holy crap!" and leaps to his feet. He swings the T-shirt that was balled up under his head, swatting his chest and back.

I rest my hands on my knees to catch my breath. "Fire ants?" I gasp, squinting at him through the sweat and sun.

"It sure-as-shit wasn't a bad dream." He flips the waistband of his jeans and picks a couple of ants out. "Actually," he says, one corner of his mouth going up, "the dream was pretty sweet." He ambles over and turns his back to me. "Mind checking me out, Snowflake?"

Reddish hair streaked with blond hangs long behind his ears. His surfer-tan back is crosshatched with the imprint of grass. He's half a foot shorter than I am, but ripped. His pants ride so low I can see that ridge of muscle Greek sculptors were so crazy about.

I don't need this. After PE I always dress fast, avoid the showers. "You look ant-free to me," I say, falling back a step.

"Shit fire!" he yelps again. "Check out the left shoulder blade."

I try to brush the ant away. It won't brush. It won't flick. When I pull it off, it leaves a spot of blood.

The guy snaps the T-shirt again, engulfing me in his personal odors—deodorant, cigarettes, and something faintly minty—the guy equivalent of Annie's perfume cloud. "Thanks, Snowflake."

I'm about to tell him my name's not Snowflake when a voice like the squeal of a marker on a white board rips the air. "Oh, boys?" Mrs. Zelinsky's torso juts out the open door of the house next to Mr. Traynor's. "Boys?" She waggles a finger at us. "Can you two help me with a little job?"

I know resistance is futile, so I trot over.

"Thank you, Fisher," she says, patting my arm. She looks over at the fire-ant victim and tickles the air with her index finger. "You too. I'll make it worth your while."

I've cut her grass for years. "Worth your while" means a glass of milk and a stale cookie—if you're lucky.

The guy plunges his arms through the sleeves of his T-shirt and flips the back of the shirt over his head. "What kind of little job?"

Mrs. Z's smile shows off the twin spots of lipstick on her teeth. "Just a couch I need moved to the curb." She holds the door for us.

13

"Forget to pay the light bill?" the guy asks as we follow her inside.

The place is funhouse-dark. It creeped me out when I was little. I turned down plenty of milk and cookies just so I wouldn't have to go in there to get them.

"Where exactly is this couch?" the guy asks as we stumble through the gloom.

Mrs. Z grips the stair rail. "Right up here."

"And how're we supposed to get it down these stairs without starting an avalanche?" he asks. On either end of each tread is a tall stack of newspapers separated by a path just wide enough for Mrs. Z's slippers to rest side by side.

"I'm sure you'll manage." She leads us into a cramped bedroom and shoos three cats off a balding couch.

The guy fans the air. "You could use a little air freshener in here."

"It's the couch," she says with an indignant huff. "Tiddles has little accidents sometimes."

He closes one eye and sights along the top of the couch. He paces its length, then does the same to the doorway. "That door is wicked narrow. There's a good chance the couch'll get stuck in the turn going into the hall. We're talking major grunt work. That'll cost you extra."

Oh, goody. *Two* cookies.

The guy hooks his thumbs through his belt loops and hikes up his jeans. "Ya ready, Snowflake?"

"Fisher," I say, holding out my hand. "My name is Fisher Brown."

"Lonny Traynor." Instead of taking my hand he grabs my forearm with a slap. My fingers close over a blue snake tattoo. "Mexico," he says, seeing me checking out the snake. "Seemed like a good idea at the time."

We stay limb-locked so long it seems meaningful, like now we'd have to die for each other if the situation called for it. And I realize I've had more skin contact with this guy in ten minutes than I've had with Hofstra in ten years. Before letting go, he gives one last hard squeeze. Then he holds out a pack of cigarettes. I shake my head no, but he lights one for himself. When Mrs. Z objects he mutters, "Smells better than the other odors you got goin'." He closes an eye against the rising smoke. The cigarette bobs with each word. "Okay, Fish. You take the dog-end."

I'm not crazy about walking down the stairs backwards, but Lonny seems to be in charge. We lift on three, then flip the couch on its back. While I shuffle toward a door I can't see, Lonny walks his end sharply left, angling the couch so that the legs go first. The legs are barely through the door when he swings the couch ninety degrees and swivels its length out into the hall.

"Watch the banister!" Out of the corner of my eye I see Mrs. Z press a hand to her heart. "It's solid oak!"

Just as I step down I hear a yowl. One of Mrs. Z's cats has inserted itself under my foot. I skip sideways to avoid crushing essential organs and accidentally nudge the top stack of newspapers. An ominous whispering quickly grows to a loud murmur; the sound of a gathering avalanche.

"Stop them!" shouts Mrs. Z. "They're all in order, by date!"

"Sorry, Mrs. Zelinsky." Over my shoulder I watch as the paper slide gains momentum. What started with a few papers is becoming a juggernaut. As each sliding stack rushes over the papers below, more break loose. When the cascade encounters the wall where the staircase hooks left, it stops for a moment, then almost imperceptibly starts to move again. The flow makes the turn, riffling down the last three stairs.

"Nice," says Lonny, nodding appreciatively.

"Nice," I agree. The whole thing is almost art.

At the top of the stairs Mrs. Z is hanging butt-up over the rail, moaning about her complete collection.

"Use 'em to paper train a few of your cats," Lonny suggests. That's when I notice that he's leaning back, muscles tense, blue snake straining. He's the only reason the couch and I didn't make the trip down the stairs along with the newspapers.

I try to imagine Hofstra or Raleigh restraining a runaway couch, but they're only heroic in joystick-controlled situations. "Thanks," I say. "I'm good to go."

Bullets of cold sweat pour down my sides as we lift the couch over the rail to make the turn, but I hold my end steady. Lonny and I slalom down the last four stairs on a complete collection of *Tallahassee Democrats*.

Mrs. Z makes her way down the stairs carefully, stopping to replace a few issues.

"Sometime today?" calls Lonny when we stand in front of the door. "This thing isn't getting any lighter."

She sprints ahead and pulls the door open, sweeping it wide and sucking in her gut.

When we drop the couch at the curb, Lonny holds up a hand for a high-five. "Hey, you're stronger than you look, Snowflake."

We've just slapped flesh when Mrs. Z gives us a "Thank you, boys" and the door begins to close. Forget the stale cookie, the glass of milk.

But Lonny skips up the short driveway and catches the edge of the door just before it shuts. "Excuse me, ma'am. Did you forget it's pay-up time?"

"Of course," she says. "Cookies?"

"The bill for today comes to fifteen dollars."

She takes a long look at the tattoo and scuffs off to find her purse. She meekly counts out a five, nine ones, and a pile of dimes and pennies.

It's the pennies that get to me. "Keep my half," I tell her.

"Thanks, Fish," says Lonny, and all the money disappears into the pocket of his jeans.

Dad's wearing his man apron, the one that says **B-B-Q KING** across the chest. Kneeling on the linoleum, he's sponging off the old plaid suitcase that usually sits on a beam in the attic. "You're late, Fisher." The table is already set. Dinner rattles the lid of the pot on the stove.

17

"Tutoring." I lift the lid. Steam from the chicken stew fogs my glasses. "Plus, I had to move Mrs. Z's couch."

"Sounds like a big job. Why didn't you come get me?"

"The guy who's been hanging out at Mr. Traynor's helped."

The sponge quits circling. Dad looks up. "That's Dave Traynor's younger brother. Dave hadn't seen him for years. He just showed up on his doorstep a few days ago. Dave says he's kind of wild."

"Wild? Most of the times I've seen him he's been asleep."

Dad rinses the sponge and squeezes it into the sink. "How'd the chem exam go?"

"Think I did okay." Feeling the fear again, I almost tell Dad about the brain lock. As a guidance counselor I bet he's seen it before. It probably even has a scientific name. But Dad looks so hopeful—the way my old dog Barney did when I picked up his leash—I decide against ruining his mood. "I'll know before you hit the road."

Dad tears off a paper towel and begins drying the suit-case. "I wish I could put this trip off until you could come along."

"That's okay, Dad."

He was planning to wait for the end of the school year to move Nana into assisted living; then a week ago she called because she couldn't remember how to turn the light off in the pantry. Needing light switch advice is even worse than needing to watch the stewardess demonstrate how to buckle your seatbelt.

"You sure you'll be okay?" he asks for the fifty-ninth time.

"Sure, fine."

Dad drops the paper towel in the garbage can and washes his hands. Then he picks up one of the bowls from the table. He spoons stew into it and passes it to me. I hand him the other one.

Now we'll say grace, eat, talk about something cheerful like SATs. I'll offer to do the dishes, but he'll say, "I'll take care of it, son, you study." From my desk upstairs I'll hear the sound of running water.

There's never a dirty dish in the sink at our house, not even a fork. Mom was the one who let dishes pile up. With Dad in charge, everything is under control.

![Chapter number 2]

uzzzzzz… I knock the alarm off the bedside table. It lies in the dark having a conniption. *Buzzzzzz…*

I groan, "Die, sucker!" and hang over the side of the bed, searching blindly. When the clock quivers in my hand I mash the OFF button. Still holding it, I flop back up onto the bed. It'd be so easy to go back to sleep hugging this clock, but I can't afford another breakdown—especially not on the SATs. It's brutal, but by falling out of bed at five I can cram in a couple more hours of study. I throw my legs over the side.

I snap my desk lamp on—and confront Dad's array of index cards. *What is the real question?* is just the most recent. Also on the windowsill: *Challenging reading in a variety of disciplines increases academic success,* and my personal favorite, *Read above and below target area (five lines each way).* I don't turn around, but I know it's there: a swarm of test tips taped to all vertical surfaces. Dad's only trying to help, but some days I feel like a sock puppet with his hand inside.

I break out the Barron's. While enlarging my vocabulary, I hear Dad downstairs in the kitchen going through his morning routine—which will segue to his work routine, followed by his evening routine.

I slide the bottom desk drawer open quietly and run a finger over the dribble of blue paint inside. Mom used to do her artwork at this desk. Like the graffiti tagger's scrawl, it's illegible. All it says for sure is, I was here.

"You're up bright and early. Did you see the tip?"

I ram the drawer in and swivel the chair. Stealth-Dad managed to open the door without a sound. "Yeah, I saw it. It's kind of hard to miss."

"Analyze before answering," he explains, in case I didn't get it.

"I figured."

"Well, I guess I'm off to school." He says it like there's some other possible course of action. "Have a nice day, son!" He's not being ironic. Dad has never perfected irony, let alone sarcasm. He one hundred percent means it. With his round, bald head he even looks like the Smiley Face.

"You too, Dad." I close the book. Time to hit my own routine: dress, eat, and catch the bus.

"Hey, Snowflake," Lonny yells. He's lying on Mrs. Z's discarded couch. Ensconced. That would be the preferred word from the SAT prep book. Lonny is *ensconced* on Mrs. Z's discarded couch. The boom box on the ground beside him is blasting an oldies station: *You CAN'T…always GET…what you WA-AAANT.*

"You ever been to Uruguay?" he shouts.

"Not lately." Uruguay? Home to school, school to home; my life is a Möbius strip, a continuous loop that goes nowhere. Bus Number 47 rounds the corner. The air brakes grunt. The opening door folds—and it's time to loop.

"You ever skip?" Lonny calls.

I put a foot on the bottom step. He cranks the volume up a couple hundred decibels, and Mick Jagger kicks me in the back of the head. *Nuh-oh, you CAN'T…always GET…what you WA-AANT… But if you try some time…just might find…ya get whatcha NEEEEED.*

The stink of puke and gym socks, erasers, and Cheetos engulfs me. The bus driver Lynelle closes the door, hits the gas, and starts right in on me. "I still don't get why you don't ride with your dad."

"My dad's the guy who brews the coffee in the teacher's lounge." I fall into my usual spot two seats behind her. "He gets there before the crack of dawn, remember?"

"Still, a junior riding the bus is sad."

I talk back to the face in the rearview mirror. "A junior who rides the bus instead of carpooling with his dad scores some extra sleep." Or would if he didn't study 24/7.

I'm wondering why I always sit up front when someone at the back of the bus whimpers, "Quit it, okay? You're hurting my arm." Now I remember. Geeks who sit in the back get broken down for parts. I close my eyes to avoid more comments from Lynelle.

The bus lurches, then lets out a high-pitched *squeeeeeal* as Lynelle brings Number 47 to a classic sliding stop. Tamika, Lataysia, and Shondra shimmy up the metal steps, giggling. Trudging up the steps behind them, shoulders hunched beneath her heavy pack, is Desiree.

"Morning, sunshine," says Lynelle.

"Hi." Desiree's pack hits the floor by my sneakers.

I surreptitiously check out her hand. Dez draws her moods on her skin. When she's happy the design curls and loops. Today's pattern is as jagged as a lightning bolt. She presses the end of her thick red braid against her lips and watches her sister, who's still on the sidewalk flirting with half a dozen guys.

"Precious, honey?" Lynelle drums her fingers on the wheel. "Would you and the boys care to join us?" Desiree's fourteen-year-old sister undulates toward the bus, setting the guys in motion.

"I told her to change that shirt," Desiree mutters. "It makes you look slutty," she calls after Precious.

Her sister passes us without looking our way. "Isn't it kind of up to your mom to nix the scanty outfits?" I ask.

She crosses her arms over her own flat chest. "Who do you think owns the shirt?" she asks. "If I don't keep Precious in line she's going to get in trouble. The females in my family reproduce like fruit flies."

"Thanks," I say. "Nice mental image." But she has a point. Their mother, Boots, was fifteen when Dez was born—Dez was an accident. Precious just sort of happened too; you'd think after one accident Boots would've figured it out. Dez has always taken care of her sister. Frankly, Dez lost control when Precious grew boobs, but she hangs on. And she plans to keep doing it. Dez has the brains and grades to go anywhere, but when the rest of our group leaves Tallahassee for top-tier colleges, she'll take the Bright Futures scholarship she and 80 percent of the graduating class will qualify for. She'll go to FSU and live at home so she can keep an eye on Precious. What a waste.

While Precious flirts in the back of the bus, Dez wraps her oversized black sweater around herself. Her head rocks against the seat, and she stares at the deep gouges in the ceiling. When she notices that I'm looking at her, she turns away.

In elementary the kids called her Troll. The latest: chin-challenged. She has a chin—but it's minimal. Some gene set randomly failed to express itself. To me it's no big deal; it's just the way she is.

I'm no great specimen either. Thick glasses, beady eyes, skinny, bony, pale. When it comes to looks, both of us are way down the slippery slope of the bell curve—okay, maybe I'm a little closer to the fat part of that curve, but not much. It's harder on a girl, I guess, especially when there are Annie Cagneys around for comparison.

"Dez?" I slide a finger under her braid and tug. "You okay?"

She shrugs, then takes out her marker and begins adding more spikes to the back of her hand. "Beanzy's sick."

I should have guessed her mood was dog related. "She's old, Dez. At least thirteen, probably older."

When we were in kindergarten, Dez's family lived on our street. For our fifth birthdays our moms took us to the animal shelter. I chose a wiggly brown puppy Mom and I named Barney. Dez latched onto an adult dog with nubby fur and crossed eyes.

Her mom begged her to trade for something cuter, but Desiree held on tight. Boots was about to go along when the shelter woman mentioned the fee to cover shots and spaying. Boots peeled Desiree's arms off the dog and tried to drag her toward the exit, but Dez grabbed the leg of the receptionist's desk and hung on, screaming at the top of her lungs.

Boots gave in and wrote a bad check.

Neither Boots nor Precious understands Dez's dedication to "that smelly old dog." But it's simple: Dez is loyal. To them, to me, to Beanzy. And none of us deserves it, except the dog. "What's wrong with the Beaner?" I ask.

"Her chest is bubbling."

"Anything in the book about bubbling?"

"I didn't look it up yet," she whispers. The marker is still going strong; the spikes on her hand have sprouted spikes.

That initial round of shots and spaying were the only vet care Beanzy ever received. When the dog gets sick, Dez diagnoses and treats with the help of a book from the pet store.

"Bubbling, bubbling..." I drum my fingers on my lips as if consulting my vast store of veterinary knowledge. "Sounds like a cold." But I'm bluffing. Suddenly, someone whoops at the back of the bus. I turn and Lou is squirting lighter fluid at the ceiling; Gonzo Franky is lighting it. "Hey, check it out." I figure the flaming ceiling will distract her, but when she turns that's not what she sees. She sees D'Andre in the back seat with his arm around her sister.

"Get your hand off my sister's boob!" she screeches. I have to grab her to keep her from storming the back of the bus, where she would be killed.

Probably by her sister.

Dez stares at my forehead. "Broccoli?"

"Not even close—you're thinking too healthy."

Dez and I are hanging out in the media center, waiting to go to first period. She has a copy of *The Great Gatsby* open on the table, but she's not reading it. I haven't even unzipped my pack. Instead, we're taking turns reading each other's minds. We invented this game so long ago it goes by the lame name of "Read My Head."

Today's category: food. I'm projecting pepperoni pizza, which she is majorly not getting.

"Count Chocula?" One more wrong guess and I'll score the point for this round.

Just then the door behind Dez opens and Annie Cagney wanders in looking beautiful and clueless. The thought bubble over her head reads: Where am I?????

Dez moves to catch my eye, blocking my view of Annie. "Well, is it?"

"You're as cold as the Pleistocene." I lean out so Annie can see me. You'd think she'd notice. She cried all over me in this very room less than fifteen hours ago, but she drifts past our table, oblivious. Never taking my eyes off her, I turn and straddle the chair. She lights at a table on the other side of the room. I focus on the crucial spot on the back of her sweater.

"I can read your head right now," Dez says. "You're lusting after Annie Cagney."

"I am not lusting. And how do you know Annie Cagney?" I know how she knows, but I have to deflect her attention from my lusting.

"Choir. She's the girl I keep telling you about, the one who stands below me on the risers. She drags the whole soprano section flat. Mouse and I call her 'The Void.' There's no brain behind that face. How do *you* know her?"

"Tutoring." Annie twists a strand of hair around her finger, then uncoils and smooths it. She twists and smooths, torturing the same piece of hair for a full minute. She acts like she and Ramos are still on the outs. "There's a dance Friday night, right?" I ask Dez.

"I think so…."

I slump over my arms, still watching Annie. Dez slaps the back of my head, "Go on. Ask her."

"What was *that* for?" I try to sound innocent, which is hard, considering she just read my head. "Ask who what?"

"Her. The Void. Ask her to the dance."

"I *wasn't* going to ask her." But I was. At least I was thinking about it. Annie's dumb, but she's beautiful—and I'm a guy. Besides, I have a theory. This is all an act, like she's playing the lead in a blonde joke. One day she'll just start talking about Plato's *Republic,* or speciation, or cold fusion.

She tosses her hair over her shoulders and wanders back out of the media center. It doesn't look like today's the day.

When the door has fully eclipsed Annie, I turn back to Dez. "Guess again."

Dez stares into her book. "I'm not playing any more."

"And Desiree Swanson defaults. Score one for Fisher Brown." Using my finger, I make another mark on the invisible scorecard in the air. "Pepperoni pizza."

She bites her lip and keeps reading.

"I wasn't going to ask her. Swear to God." Under the table, I bump Dez's knee with mine. "Talk to me, Dez. Isn't this, like, your third time around with Jay Gatsby? You already know how it ends."

"Maybe I'm hoping it'll be different this time." She raises the book so that her face is completely hidden.

"Different how?" When she doesn't answer, I launch my attack. Random objects, nudged across the table, begin to appear beneath the edge of her raised book: an eraser, a chewed stub of pencil, a scrap of paper with the words "Earth to Dez" scribbled on it. I strain across the table to slip a hand between her eyes and the page and wiggle my fingers. With a huff, she swivels in her chair.

Now that her back is to me I can read the pages too, so I do—in my most annoying falsetto.

"'As he left the room again she got up and went over to

Gatsby, and pulled his face down kissing him on the mouth. "You know I love you," she murmured.'"

I tip back in my chair. "Yeah, yeah, and they all live happily ever after."

"No they don't!" Dez whips around. "Gatsby dies in less than a hundred pages!"

"Maybe that was just the last time you read it." I'm joking, but I have to admit, I'm surprised. "Hey, why don't you quit reading now while he's ahead? When I ditched the book, Gatsby was doing fine."

She thrusts one arm through a pack strap and hugs the book protectively with the other. "How can anyone *not* finish *The Great Gatsby?*"

"Priorities. I had a huge bio project due that week." I grab my own pack. "Besides, it's not like I'm taking the AP English exam."

"You think that's why a person reads books, to score big on tests?"

I follow her into the hall. "Uh…yes?"

"You are so shallow! You are Daisy Buchanan with a Y chromosome."

"Wow. A scientific-slash-literary putdown; I'm impressed. But I don't get it. Let's see, I vaguely remember a character named Daisy—no wait, that was Daisy Duke."

She lifts her eyes to the ceiling. "God. If you exist, smite him. Do it now." But when she looks at me again, all the pissed-offness is gone. She wants me to understand. "Reading isn't about taking tests," she says quietly. "It's about—flying."

I hate it when she gets all symbolic on me. "You think

because I don't read novels I don't fly? There are other ways, Dez."

"Sure there are," she says, facing me. "You choose your wings. Tell me, Fisher. What wings do you choose?"

I cross my arms. "Read my head."

"Have a nice day, Fisher." When Dad says this, it's a pat on the back. When Dez says it, it's like she's taken the words apart and sharpened the edges. Irony. Sarcasm. She had them down cold by second grade.

"Hey, you too." I hope she catches the return sarcasm, but she quickly disappears into the crowd stampeding to the second floor. I head for the Nettles Building.

And another "nice" day at Leon High begins.

"Surrender, goddamn it." Last bell has rung, there's no big hurry. I kick the locker door anyway, to establish who's boss. I spin the dial for the fourth time, hit the magic numbers, and...*again*, nothing happens.

Dez walks up. Sometime during the day she twisted her braid into a knot and stuck a pencil through it. She looks like an overworked middle-aged librarian—which is what she's practicing to be; Dez is close to a world record for community service hours at a public library. She opens the locker next to mine in 3.2 seconds.

I step away from mine. "Listen, do you mind?"

For a second she stands with her eyes closed, her forehead against her locker door, probably asking the god she doesn't believe in to give her strength.

"I know, I'm helpless, but my wings are in there. I have to get them if I'm going to fly."

She punches my shoulder, but she reaches over and spins the dial on my lock. The door opens in one try. "What's the problem with you and this lock?"

"It hates me." I grab a couple of books and slam the door. "You're staying after for Dad's SAT practice session, aren't you?"

"Can't. I have to drive Boots to the doctor."

"She still can't drive?"

"Of course she can drive. She can't be *seen* driving."

The accident happened three weeks ago. The car wouldn't start, so Boots took Taltran to her job at Seminole Subs. The bus lurched. She hit her shoulder. She had an ice pack on it when she turned on the TV and met personal injury attorney Dexter Lazarus, who gave his personal guarantee, *"You* don't pay unless *I* collect."

"It's too bad you'll miss SAT practice, Dez."

"No big deal. I'll kick butt on verbal and I won't embarrass myself on math."

"I could help you get ready for math."

"Why? My score'll be good enough for where I'm going."

I follow her out the front door. "Quit limiting yourself. Wings, Dez, wings!"

She gives me a back-of-the-hand wave as she climbs the metal stairs—somehow I've trailed her all the way to the bus.

Lynelle raises her unibrow. "In or out?"

"I'll tutor you," I repeat, ignoring the bus driver. "Gratis."

"Aren't you too busy tutoring The Void?" Dez calls.

"Forget I offered. Have a nice day." I shove my hands deep into my pockets and walk back toward the school.

When I walk into the media center where the test is being given, Hofstra and Raleigh are flipping a hacky sack while they wait for the practice test to begin. "Heads up, Fisher." Hofstra zings the sack at me; I pop it over to Raleigh.

Raleigh juggles it with his feet. He plays soccer—another smart academic move. He flips the sack back to me. I flail at it with a knee and connect. "Stellar shot," he says when it nails Hofstra in the middle of his forehead. The three blondes in the corner giggle.

Hofstra catches the sack in his hand and bows. "Are they laughing at me or with me?" he asks out of the side of his mouth.

"At," says Raleigh. "Definitely at."

Dad flicks the lights. "Seats, people."

Raleigh pockets the hacky sack. Still grinning at the girls, Hofstra collapses into his seat.

Dad places a sample test in front of each student. "Your test must remain face down until I give the signal." Practically salivating, the geeks pick up their pencils. But there's a disturbance. "Ladies…," Dad warns the blonde quadrant of the room.

The whispering goes on. Finally one girl blurts out, "Steph doesn't have a pencil."

In what is possibly the slickest move of his life, Hofstra tosses a pencil to Steph, who sits at a table in the opposite corner of the room. She catches it and smiles at him.

"Shit," mutters Raleigh. "I had an extra pencil."

Steph is instantly back in her own galaxy, but Hofstra is grinning like a fool—not a good look for a guy with lunch in his braces.

"Remember," Dad says, "there is a guessing penalty." Then he drops one of the helpful hints already enshrined on an index card in my room. "If you can eliminate two of the answers, go ahead and guess. But don't Christmas tree. And don't forget to fill in your name; it's worth two hundred points." He directs the last comment toward Steph and company. "All right. Go."

I turn the test over and discover that today's half is math. Sweet. After yesterday's meltdown I can use a gimme. SAT I math only covers the easy stuff like arithmetic, algebra up to the quadratic formula, linear equations, numerators, order of operations, plane and coordinate geometry—I'll blow this baby out of the water.

The test finished forty-five minutes ago, but after we'd each scored our own, the geeks (plus Dad) went around coaching the mathematically less fortunate. I helped Joe and Sean, a couple of guys I tutor. Because she used his pencil, Hofstra claimed Steph. For half an hour straight, he performed math like a kid popping wheelies, then followed her out the door.

Dad and I are the last to leave the media center. The last, in fact, to leave the school. Aboard the *Titanic,* Dad would have been the guy playing violin as the ship went down.

"How'd you do?" he asks as our footsteps reverberate in the empty hall.

"Missed a couple."

He stops. "Did the *math* give you a problem?"

"No way," I assure him. "I just got sloppy—read a couple numbers wrong."

Dad blasts me with a look of concern. "You don't want to let things slide again."

"Again? That was sixth grade, Dad." Sixth grade was my watershed year, my Armageddon. It was the year Mom left. Until then I had always been an average student, sliding by, doing the minimum. After, I took underachieving to a whole new level. But by now even Dad has to know I'm past the danger zone. "Can we get out of here? If we don't move it, we'll meet ourselves coming the other way."

His loafers make an aggravating *tappy tap* against the linoleum. "You seemed to have extra time." Meaning, I should have gone back and checked.

"Yeah, well, it's not like it counts." I don't tell him, but I *did* check. Somehow I still messed up. Getting the same queasy feeling I had during the chem exam, I let him walk on ahead of me.

Seen from behind, Dad looks suddenly smaller than usual, his shoulders stooped. My wrong answers may be what's shrinking him now, but I won't take the blame for the sagging shoulders. Mom did that.

I remember coming home from my scout meeting the day she left and finding Dad hunched over the pot of spaghetti sauce he was stirring, like whatever had made him stand straight had broken.

I didn't believe him when he told me she was gone for good. It wasn't the first time she'd left. When he insisted, I went ballistic. "Why?" I kept yelling at his Quasimodo back. I still remember his explanation. He said Mom was like a moth that flies toward a light bulb, mistaking it for something more.

I didn't get it. Wouldn't she see it was just a stupid light bulb and come home?

But she didn't.

That's when I discovered I had a lot in common with Ramos Cruz. His mom lived with him, but his dad had split. Left back twice, Ramos was the biggest kid in the class, but only an inch taller than me. Sitting together in the last row, we got in so much trouble I was in danger of flunking sixth.

Dad had me transferred to another class where I had zero friends. In the last quarter I won the award for *most improved*. By the end of seventh, a straight-A report card was routine. Dad was one happy camper.

As long as I'm the A man, we're okay. In his mind we've survived Mom's desertion. Faulty logic, but it's a prime reason why I work so hard. It seems like the least I can do for him.

That doesn't mean I don't zone him out sometimes. "Blah, blah, alert, blah, careful, blah, blah, real test," he frets as we walk past the main office. I stop and act interested in the glass case of trophies. "You are quite capable of a perfect score, quite capable," he declares.

Am I? What if for all these years I've been *over*achieving—literally running my brain beyond its capacity? Suddenly I feel dead tired. "Look, Dad. Here's a trophy from the football team of 1951. I wonder if any of these guys are still alive."

His smile's apologetic. "Do I detect a change of subject?"

"Could be." He puts a hand on my back. "Don't worry, Dad. I'll do better on the real test."

"Over here, Fisher!" Desiree jumps down off the trunk of her mother's Crown Vic, waving her arms, just as Dad steps out the back door of the school.

"I've been waiting for you, Fisher. Get in the car!"

"I'm sure he has homework—" Dad starts.

"Please, Mr. Brown? I'm taking Beanzy to the park. Fisher needs some fresh air too. Look how pale he is. It's like he lives under a rock."

Car key in hand, Dad hesitates, checking me for fungoid tendencies. He's going to say yes. Dad likes Dez. "One hour, then you have to bring him home. Deal?"

"Deal." She smiles. Then she yells, "Move it, Fisher!"

"Don't I have any say?" I protest, but I'm glad to get away from Dad's disappointment. I'm jogging toward the Vic when I have to jump back. A red jeep that is barreling for the exit tries to run me down. Inside are Annie and Ramos.

Ramos must have stayed after for some athletic sweatfest; Annie stayed to watch him sweat. Seeing them cohabit the front seat makes me madder at Dad.

"Missed a couple lousy questions on the practice test," I grumble as I slide under the wheel and across the velvet upholstery—both doors on the Vic's passenger side were permanently sealed when Boots sideswiped a telephone pole. "Two wrong, and Dad's all over me."

"At least he cares." Dez does great in school but Boots doesn't notice. She's more into Precious, who's bagging Cs and Ds but growing up a first class babe.

Dez's dark red hair is loose now. It cascades over her shoulders as she kneels in the driver's seat to check the dog in the backseat. I almost say "nice hair" but come out with "I see the librarian bun is gone" because Dez and I communicate through insults. "Which park?"

"San Pedro. We're taking her to the dog run."

"Going to sniff a few butts, eh, Beanzy?" I roll my window as far down as it will go in the smashed door. "Have at it, Beaner. Stick your head out and let the spit fly." But this time Dez's dog doesn't hang her paws over the back of my seat and grin into the wind. She lies perfectly still. Something way worse than a cold is wrong with her dog, but except for the spiky black design that has metastasized up her arm, Dez isn't talking about it. I prop a size fourteen on the dash. "How'd the appointment go?"

"Not great." She turns the key. We both hold our breath until the engine coughs to life. "The doctor told Mom her shoulder is fine." Dez grasps the juddering wheel with both hands and stomps the pedal. "No shoulder injury, no big set-tlement," she declares.

"There goes the cruise to the Bahamas."

Dez thrusts her arm out the window to signal. "There goes the private island." Strands of hair leap wildly around her face, like flames, obscuring her lack of chin. For one moment, Dez is beautiful.

She gathers her hair in one hand, bringing it back into control. "The dance on Friday night, you want to go?" The Vic swims wide around a turn and enters the park.

"Sure," I say. "Why not?" No chance of asking Annie now. She's gone back to being Ramos's appendage. "I'll round up Hofstra and Raleigh. You think Mouse'd like to come? She seemed to enjoy the last social experiment." Nor-mally, none of us go to school dances, but last fall Dez sug-gested we drop in on the homecoming dance as social anthropologists studying the courtship rituals of the natives.

"Wasn't once enough with the social experiment thing?" she asks. "Hofstra made a total fool of himself."

"He danced like a wild man, so what? Think about the way you and I danced." I was all for holding up the wall, but Dez insisted we get out there. Given the fact I'm a foot and a half taller than she is, there were mechanical difficulties. She stood on her toes. Knuckles dragging, I did the Franken-stein. I was ready to give up when she put a foot on top of each of my sneakers.

"It was fun!"

"It was embarrassing." Raleigh called what we were doing Daddy Dancing.

"I'll tell you what was embarrassing—Hofstra barfing on his shoes in the parking lot."

"Too much beer. I'll keep him straight this time, okay?"

"Why don't we go together, just the two of us?" she asks, staring at the road.

"You mean like…a date?"

"A date?" She glances at me, then looks away. "Can't we just go? Do we have to call it something?"

"Well…uh…" I run a finger along a gritty seam in the upholstery. The thing is, her, me…it will *look* like a date, and if it *looks* like a date….

"Forget it," she says.

"Consider it forgotten." In a little while Dez starts to sing quietly, under her breath. She may not even be aware she's doing it. She sings when she's happy, or when something bothers her.

I slide down in my seat, close my eyes, and act as if the conversation never happened.

3

I t's Friday. Chem exams come back today. I should have good news for Dad before he launches for South Florida this afternoon. Except for the question I blanked on, I feel pretty solid. I'm glad I didn't tell Dad about the way my brain turned slick and everything slid off.

What's a little brain freeze compared to screwing up the whole test? Bet Hofstra's jumpy this morning.

As I load my pack I glance out the window. Lonny's on the couch again. His neck is propped on a ratty throw pillow, his ankles crossed. Hello. What's wrong with this picture? I had to think for a moment before I figured it out. He's holding a book. Hard to believe he's reading. Maybe he's using it to shade his face.

I have twenty minutes to kill before the bus rolls up. I could waste it chewing cold cereal, but I'm too worried about the test score to eat. Think I'll check out Lonny's book.

He hollers, "Hey, Fish!" as I lock the front door behind me.

"Hey, Lonny."

He kicks his legs over the side and slaps a cushion. "Have a seat, man."

I drop my pack on the ground and fall onto the sofa beside him. "What're you reading?"

"Guidebook to Uruguay." He holds it up so I can see the cover.

"In Spanish? You speak Spanish?"

"Sure. Picked it up the same place I picked up this." He taps the blue snake on his arm. "Plus, my traveling buddy was Mexican."

While I contrast learning a language among the natives with sitting in a classroom next to Hofstra declining nouns in a dead language, Lonny digs a cigarette pack from between the cushions and shakes out a couple. He pulls the cigarettes the rest of the way out with his lips, then extracts the red Bic lighter from the cellophane around the pack. He lights both cigarettes and holds one out to me.

"No thanks, I'm good—"

He bumps my hand with the back of his wrist. "Go on. You could use something to stunt your growth."

While I feel the firmness of the filter between my lips, Lonny takes a deep drag. He draws the smoke in, then lets it leak slowly out his nostrils. I know enough not to try that. I had a near-death experience once when Dez and I smoked one of Boots's cigarettes. We were about ten. I sucked that smoke in deep—then hurled. I take a shallow drag.

We smoke a while in silence. Lonny raises his eyebrows, as if that's the mechanism to open his eyelids. "You going to school again?"

"Looks like it." We lift our cigarettes to our lips. Lonny blows a few smoke rings. The man smokes as if it were a paying job.

He flicks ash over the arm of the couch, then pokes my backpack with the toe of his boot. "You study a lot?"

I shrug.

He takes a final deep drag, sucking the glow right up to the filter. "Why?"

"Got some big tests coming up. Got to get ready for college, learn the secret of life…. You know, crap like that."

He flicks his cigarette butt into the street, then looks pointedly at the one in my hand. I pass it to him.

He installs the cigarette in his mouth. Leaning forward, he jerks my pack off the ground by one strap. "It's not in here," he says as the pack twists slowly.

"What's not?"

"The secret of life." He drops it. When the pack rolls on its side, he props his feet on it.

"You don't even know what books I've got in there."

"Doesn't matter. Books are just other people telling you what they've seen."

Dez would argue him on that one—he's dissing her wings. Personally, I dispute the word "seen." Most of what I'm studying no one's ever seen. I left the concrete for the abstract a couple of years ago—maybe Lonny never got that far. And then there's the big contradiction, the book in his hand. I flick the cover with one finger. "I see you have someone telling you about Uruguay."

He tosses the book down. "This is just a preview. I'm

goin' just as soon as I can get my finances in order." He spreads his hands as if he's offering me everything that's not in books. "What're you, Fish, a junior? My junior year—right about this time, in fact—I asked my girlfriend if she'd like to see the Pacific."

I almost say "holy shit!" but I stay cool. In fact, I barely turn my head. "And she said okay?"

He expels smoke in a lazy stream. "Uh-huh."

"Really." Staying cool is becoming problematic. "Your parents were okay with it?"

"What parents?" He flicks the cigarette butt into the street. "I was sleeping on my aunt's couch. Besides, it wasn't the first time I took off. Summer before that was the Mexico trip with my buddy Mike." As proof he holds out his tattooed arm.

"If you need a snake tattoo, I guess it's worth the mileage."

"Oh, yeah, it is." I can tell by the smile that spreads across his face he's not thinking about a guy injecting ink subcutaneously. I'm more interested in the trip he took junior year, when he should have been looking at colleges, taking SATs, working on his pet ulcer. Maybe his aunt didn't care. But somebody must have. "What did your girlfriend's parents say?"

"Guess we forgot to ask them. I had wheels, she had waitress money. I coasted down her driveway with the lights out. I could see the back of her daddy's head through the window. He didn't even twitch when I signaled." Lonny cups his hands and blows into the gap between his thumbs, producing a hollow whistle. "Her room was on the second floor. She just stepped up on the sill—and jumped."

Suddenly, I see myself standing under Annie's window. I whistle—in this fantasy I know how. She jumps. Of course I'm in the wrong spot. I don't even break her fall.

But sneaking a girl out of her house isn't the only thing wrong with this scenario. At Leon, miss four unexcused days and you zero out the semester. "When you got home you slid back into school, no big deal?"

"By the time we got back, school seemed sort of beside the point."

"You dropped out?" I rake my fingers through my hair. I stop myself before I start pulling on it. "Was it worth it?"

He nods slowly. "Let me tell you, that Pacific is one damned big ocean."

"You might not have noticed, but we have one on this side of the country too. Shore to the left of the water, shore to the right. What's the difference?"

Lonny stretches his legs out stiff, squeezes a couple of fingers into the pocket of his jeans, and slides out a striated rock. "You ever seen the sun rise over the desert? You ever pack a mule to the bottom of the Grand Canyon?" He drops the rock in my hand. "It took us four months to make the West Coast. We worked odd jobs, slept under the stars. You ain't seen nothing 'til you've seen Big Sur. It's the journey, man."

I hold up the rock. "You traded a diploma for this? You could've had both. I mean, Big Sur wasn't going anywhere. You could've checked it out later."

45

"Later, Fish? When's that? Life is one piss long and then you die."

"Deep. That's Shakespeare, right?" But as I study the rock in my hand the streaks of pink, purple, and dried-blood red morph into mountains, ocean waves, a painted desert. I turn it over and over, like Gollum fondling his Precious.

I don't notice the bus until Lynelle taps the horn and bawls, "I'm not getting any younger!"

"Surprise the hell out of her," says Lonny. "Don't get on."

I don't know if anything would surprise Lynelle, but I don't test it.

Millikan circulates, randomly handing back the exams. Chaz Weinstein looks at his and groans. "Direct hit," breathes Hofstra. "God, I just want to get this over with."

The rock in my pocket presses into my thigh. I don't know how it happened, but when I fell into my seat on Number 47 it was still in my hand. Now, for a nanosecond, instead of watching my bald chemistry teacher, I see a flickering stretch of road unspooling through a windshield.

"Incoming!" warns Hofstra. Millikan is headed our way. He walks past me and Hofstra.

"Ninety-six!" yelps Raleigh as the chem test hits his desk. "Read it and weep!"

Now Millikan hovers over Hofstra. Hofstra's hands are folded so tight his knuckles are a pale green. "Mr. Hofstra." The way Millikan holds the paper a beat too long before putting it in Hofstra's hand seems significant.

All I can see above the edge of the paper are Hofstra's glasses, his pimply forehead, but Raleigh can see the grade. "You dog!" he howls. "You lying dog!"

"Unbelievable," breathes Hofstra, and the exam drops to the desk.

Aced it. He totally aced it. He didn't study, he didn't sleep the night before, and *still* he aced it. But I'll be okay. My 96 will maintain the status quo.

Millikan deals a few more papers off the pile. When he gets to mine he doesn't make eye contact. That should warn me, but when he hands it to me all I can do is stare at it. Blindsided, I can't assimilate what's in front of me. Raleigh does it for me. "Damn, Fisher. Was your head up your butt?"

I don't get it. Except for number three, I'm positive the answers are correct. I remembered the formulas; I did everything right. But after each solution Millikan has written a single word: *UNITS.* What the hell does he mean, *UNITS?* He's taken 50 percent off each answer because I failed to specify units? "Mr. Millikan, I—"

He leans over and taps one of my offending solutions. "What is it, Mr. Brown, grams, milligrams, tonnage?"

"But the units are specified in the questions!" I act indignant, but it isn't going to fly. On the long list of Millikan's Rules are the words, "specify units." And I swear, I thought I wrote them on the test. It looks like the brain freeze took out more than my ability to convert to Kelvin. I resort to begging. "Units are, like, kind of minor compared to—"

"I teach future scientists, Mr. Brown. Scientists specify units." He frowns.

47

"But 50 percent off? That's cruel and unusual!"

He looks at me like I'll thank him later. But I won't because there is no "later." I'm dead.

Millikan just torpedoed my GPA.

"Pills," suggests Raleigh. "Large quantities. It's your only way out, Fisher."

Hofstra, Raleigh, and I are at our table in the cafeteria.

"Lay off him, Raleigh." Hofstra pulls his daily bologna sandwich out of his pack. He lifts the top slice of squishy white bread and starts tearing it into pieces.

"Do you mind?" I ask.

"Mind what?" He squeezes a mayonnaise-slimed bit into a dough pill and swallows it with Coke.

"That! It's gross, okay?"

"You never minded before."

"Correction. I never *said* anything about it before."

He goes on molding dough balls and swallowing them, his Adam's apple running up and down his scrawny neck like a small animal frantic to find its way out. When he picks up a greasy slice of lunchmeat, I stagger to my feet. "What's wrong with you?" he asks, dangling the bologna just above his open mouth.

I step over the bench and head toward the nearest exit. "You could drop the class," Raleigh calls after me, like he's handing me a get-out-of-jail-free card.

But passing—no, slam-dunking—chemistry is an essential part of the plan.

"You could go somewhere else, start a new life…." Raleigh is enjoying this way too much.

I have to find Dez. She'll understand. Somewhere in the back of an old notebook is a list we started after Mom left. At the top it says: *Why Life Stinks*. Flunking on a technicality? That's one for the list.

Sometimes Dez eats on the hill in front of the school. Today she's there, but she's talking on Mouse's cell phone. Mouse is sucking on a Tootsie Roll Pop—her usual lunch.

"What's going on?" I ask.

Mouse shoves the pop into her cheek with her tongue. "Checking on Beanzy."

Ever since our walk in the park, Desiree has been calling Boots on Mouse's cell phone between classes or pumping quarters into the pay phone when she can't find Mouse.

"Wake her up," Desiree begs. "Please, Mom? Would you just do it? I'll wait." The jagged ink marks on the back of the hand that holds the phone are exploding up her arm.

I'm about to walk away when she says, "Oh god!" and hangs up with a sob. The bell rings for next period. Lifting her cell out of Dez's hand, Mouse jumps to her feet. "Hope it works out." She makes the sympathy face then darts off to class.

Which leaves me. "What's wrong, Dez?" Knees pulled up, she's crying into her skirt. I touch her shoulder. "Dez?"

"It's Bean…zyyyy." She covers her mouth with her sleeve. "Boots just found her sleeping in a puddle of pee."

Suddenly, I feel impatient. I go down in flames and she's crying over a little dog pee. "Is that really a big deal? I mean, accidents happen." Second bell rings. "Listen, we should get to class."

"So go!" She presses her face to her knees. Her shoulders shake.

"I'm still here, Dez." She doesn't answer. I shift my weight. "Idea. We take her to a vet after school. I pay."

Her head comes up, eyes shiny with tears, but she gives me a weak smile. "Really?"

"Really. After that, you can help me figure out how to kill myself painlessly."

"Okay."

I have just enough time to collect the money buried under my socks and fix a quick snack before Dez picks me up in the Vic.

I'm scarfing a whole-wheat bagel when Dad walks in. "Did someone phone in a bomb scare?" I ask. "You never leave school this early." Then I remember he is about to take off for South Florida. How could I forget? He's been packed for days, the suitcase near the door. I've heard him prowling the house in the middle of the night. Changes in routine disturb him.

"Did you get back that chemistry—?"

The phone rings. Dad picks up, then puts his glasses on top of his head and closes his eyes. "I'll get a hotel as soon as I feel tired, I promise. Yes, I'll get something to eat too." It must be Nana. There have been lots of these conversations over the last few days.

Now Dad covers the receiver and whispers, "You'd think we were planning the D-Day invasion."

I wash down the last bite of bagel with a slug of milk. "See ya, Dad. Have a safe trip."

"Wait!" Dad covers the mouthpiece again. "Where are you going?"

"Dog emergency. Dez and I are taking Beanzy to the vet." I give him a quick one-arm hug and bound out the door just as the Vic lurches up.

Dez sets the hand brake and climbs out without turning the engine off. I slide in. Beanzy lies on a striped blanket in the back seat. Her breathing is a phlegmy rattle followed by silence. When it seems as if she's stopped for good, the next breath scrapes into her lungs.

"Hi, Beaner." As Dez slides back behind the wheel, I reach over the seat and pat Beanzy. She rolls her eyes up at me, her tail quivering hello. Her legs are so swollen it looks as if someone put a hose under her skin and let it run. "What's the matter with her legs?"

Dez sobs.

"Come on, Dez. Don't cry. We're going to the miracle vet! The miracle vet cures all!" As I do a stupid little arm-waving dance a familiar stench wafts from the back seat. It takes a couple of seconds, but then I remember. Grandpa smelled that way when he was dying. He couldn't control his bladder either. The summer after Mom left, Dad and I went to Miami to help Nana take care of him. It wasn't like we were having a good time at home anyway.

"The legs have got to be a symptom of something," I say.

"The vet will take one look and he'll know what to do."

Dez just keeps repeating the address like a mantra: "Twenty-two fifty-five South Monroe; twenty-two fifty-five…." She blows right past it then does a screeching one-eighty in the middle of the road. A pickup barely misses the Vic's only functional front door.

She skids into the parking space so fast the front end of the Vic climbs the concrete stop, then *whumps* back to earth. "We're here, girl," Dez says as she springs out of the car and opens the back door. But when the dog just lies there, Dez folds her arms across her chest and holds her elbows.

"I'll carry her."

"No, you'll wreck your clothes." For the first time I notice the wet splotch on the front of Dez's skirt: dog leakage from when she carried Beanzy to the car.

"It's okay. What's a little pee between friends?"

Dez steps aside, still hugging herself. When I tug on the blanket to slide Beanzy toward the door, the dog lets out a warning growl.

"Stop it!" Desiree wails. "You're hurting her on the seat-belt buckles!"

I talk to the dog quietly. "It's okay, Beanzy. It's okay." When Grandpa was sick he used to curse every time Dad rolled him over to change the sheets—words Nana said he hadn't used since Vietnam. He just wanted to be left alone to die in peace. As I lift the dog and the soaked blanket into my arms, I think maybe that's what Beanzy wants too. But she can't. She has to live for Dez.

Desiree holds the dog's tail and we walk into the clinic. I

collapse on a bench inside the door next to a cage of puppies needing good homes. "Hey, Beanzy, check out the pups," I say, but Beanzy is too busy breathing.

The receptionist questions Desiree: Name of the dog?

"Beanzy."

Age?

"More than twelve." The receptionist glances up. Desiree explains about picking the dog for her fifth birthday present.

Shots up to date? The tears start again.

When the paperwork is done, Dez sits beside me, holding onto Beanzy's tail as healthy-looking dogs and cats are dragged or carried through the door labeled *Exam Rooms*.

Finally it's our turn. A tall, thin man with glasses sticks his head out. "Swanson?" He introduces himself as Dr. Marks.

I carry the dog to an exam room and lay her on the stainless steel table. Dez is busy rearranging paws, flopping an ear the right way. She doesn't see Dr. Marks frown. She looks up at him believing he really is the miracle vet and he can fix everything.

The vet shines a light in each of Beanzy's eyes. He checks the dog's gums, her ears. Then he casually picks up a paw and squeezes the skin just above the ankle. He sets the paw down and gives it a quick pat. "How long have her legs been swollen?"

Dez's answer is barely a whisper. "A couple of days."

"And how long has she been having problems with bladder control?"

Dez insists, "Her bladder's fine." She doesn't want to embarrass Beanzy.

"That started today," I say. "Usually, she's fine."

Dr. Marks leans against the sink behind him and crosses his arms. "The saddest thing about animals is that they don't last as long as their owners do. From the look of her, I'd guess that Beanzy has had a long, happy life."

"Had?" Desiree covers her mouth with both hands.

"I'm afraid there comes a time—"

"Just fix her, okay?" I cut him off. "Fix her. We have money."

Dr. Marks looks back and forth between us. "I'm sorry. I'd fix her if I could, but I can't." He explains slowly and deliberately. "She's in kidney failure. That's why her legs are swollen. You can take her home, try to make her comfortable, but without working kidneys she'll die a slow death. Why not make it easy for her?"

Dez whimpers.

The vet gives her a sympathetic look. "I promise you the procedure is painless. It's like going into a nice deep sleep and not waking up again. I'll leave you two alone to talk about it."

Desiree stares daggers at the door that has just closed behind the vet. "How does *he* know it's painless? Has he ever tried it on a human and asked for a report as they drift happily off?" She presses a fist to her mouth. "What are we going to do, Fisher?"

Do I have a "kick me" sign on my back? First I put a bullet in my chemistry grade, now Dez expects *me* to choose the way her dog dies. "It's your call, Dez. She's your dog."

Sobbing, she whirls and puts her arms around Beanzy. She buries her face in the nubby fur of the dog's neck. I study a diagram of the canine skeleton on the wall. When I glance over my shoulder, Dez is still holding the dog in her arms, her tears falling on Beanzy's mottled fur. I turn back to the chart fast and count dog ribs.

Behind me the door whispers open. "What have you two decided?"

"The data is strictly empirical, but it *looked* painless."

"Shut up, Fisher." She's holding the key, but not making a move to start the Vic.

"I mean, at least she didn't suffer." I'm telling the truth. The vet injected something into a vein in the top of Beanzy's paw. After a little while her nose and lips changed color. Weird, since they were black to begin with, but they gradually turned a deep navy blue. At the very end, her tongue popped out of her mouth.

At the sight of that small blue tongue, Desiree lost it. The vet engulfed her in a lab-coat hug; I studied a 3-D model of the feline heart intently like there was going to be a test. *Auricles...ventricles...*

I wish I hadn't watched Beanzy die. One second she was in there looking out through scared brown eyes—the next her eyes went blank. It was over so fast.

"Do you want us to take care of the body?" the vet asked quietly.

Dez couldn't bury her at home; the Swansons live in a rental. I was sure she'd say yes and we'd walk away.

But Dez never does anything the easy way. "No!" she wailed. "Beanzy is coming with us."

That meant I had to carry the dog out. I wrapped the body carefully in the wet blanket so none of it showed, then forced my arms under it. Dead, Beanzy seemed heavier, off balance. When her head flopped out of the blanket it scared the shit out of me. I thought she'd come back to life.

Even though it didn't matter anymore, I tried to avoid the seat-belt buckles as I dragged the blanket to the middle of the seat. I offered to drive. Dez said no.

"One of us should drive," I say. She looks at the key in her hand as if she doesn't know what it is, then slowly inserts it in the ignition.

When the Vic doesn't start, her hands fall in her lap. I'm ready to climb out the window and jiggle the wires—anything to get this over with—but Dez shoulders the door open and staggers out of the car. For a second the hood blocks my view. *Squeak, squeak,* metal scrapes metal. The hood slams.

She drops back into the seat and turns the key. The engine farts, and the Vic thumps out of the parking lot.

I glance over my shoulder at the bundle in the backseat. "We should probably…you know…bury her."

Dez stretches the end of her sleeve over her palm and blots her eyes, but she seems to be listening.

"We could drive out Springhill Road and bury her in the national forest."

Suddenly, and for no apparent reason, she picks this moment to start crying uncontrollably. I have to grab the wheel. "Pull over," I yell, "right now!"

Forget the entrance ramp. She whumps over the curb at the Dollar Store, hits the brakes, and stalls out. The only sound in the car is the sobby catch of each breath as she tries to stop crying.

I trade places with her, taking over the wheel. Not knowing where else to go, and getting no response out of Dez, I head for my house. At least Dad will be gone—the only bright spot in the day being that I won't have to tell him about the test.

But when we pull into the driveway Dad is just setting his suitcase in the trunk of the Nissan. Without closing the trunk lid he rushes over to the passenger window. Desiree rolls it down as far as it will go. "How is your—?" His eyes settle on the bundle in the back seat. "Oh, I see." He squeezes one hand with the other. "I'm so sorry."

He looks at me like I'm supposed to do something. Why does everyone think I know what to do? When I just sit there he turns back to Dez. "Do you have someplace special to bury her?"

She draws a shaky breath. "No sir."

I'm reading Dad's head. Our backyard is small and he has every inch planned for some gardening project or other. Barney, buried with his favorite ball and squeaky bone, is already taking up valuable garden space. Plus, Dad should be on the road headed for south Florida right now, not planting dogs.

He drums his thumb against his lip, then stops. "We can bury her here if you like. There's a perfect spot in the back-yard."

Desiree shoves me out of the car. She runs to Dad and throws herself at him. "Thank you, thank you!"

When it comes to hugging or getting hugged, Dad is out of practice. "Happy to do it," he stammers, giving her back a hesitant pat.

I look away—and there's Lonny across the street smoking a cigarette. The couch is gone; Bulk Trash made a pickup this morning. He squats on his heels. "What ya got there?" he yells when Dad and I drag the blanket out.

"A dead dog," I yell back. A sob chokes Desiree. Dad, who's carrying the front end of the load, turns and stares at me.

I get it. I'm tactless. But I'm not having a great day either.

"When I get back we'll plant flowers to mark the spot," Dad says, stepping on the shovel. "You can choose the kind." Wishing he'd talk less and dig more, I glance at the bundle of dead dog on the ground. He tosses a shovelful of dirt. "Visit her whenever you like." He keeps talking while he digs, but the words can't cover what he's doing—there aren't enough of them.

I offer to take a turn, but Dad won't surrender the shovel. Instead he nods toward Desiree, who seems to be having a hard time staying on her feet. What's he trying to tell me? He can't expect me to put my arm around her. If he's out of practice when it comes to hugging or being hugged, I'm an island that has yet to be discovered. I stand around and listen to sand grit against the shovel.

Finally, finally, a hole for a thirty-pound dog gapes in the grass.

Dad and I lower Beanzy. Desiree opens the blanket and leans into the hole to kiss the dead dog.

"I'll take over, Dad. You should go." But Dad is thorough. He shovels the dirt back into the hole. Together he and Dez arrange clumps of grass over the grave like a shaggy patchwork quilt. Dad does better when Dez flings herself at him again—doesn't stagger or anything.

It's *his* arm that's around her shoulders as we walk her to her car. I trail uselessly a few feet behind them and stop by Dad's Nissan. It's Dad who gets the car door for Dez. And when the Vic's engine chokes, it's Dad who pops the hood and jiggles the wires.

I can see Lonny's silhouette, the glowing tip of his cigarette. Like me he's probably thinking, the Vic is running fine. Why doesn't she drive away?

Then Dad can drive away.

Then I can spend the rest of the night in my room studying—a lousy end to a lousy day.

Killing time, I turn and stare into the Nissan's open trunk. Dad's suitcase crouches next to the spare. Even without seeing him pack, I know exactly what's inside: white boxers, crew socks, a half dozen cotton shirts he ironed before packing—which he will iron again before wearing—khakis, a second pair of brown loafers.

Why is Desiree's departure not happening? I take a quick glance. Dad is passing her his spare handkerchief through the window of the Vic.

I rest my forehead on the cool edge of the trunk lid and notice that next to the suitcase is a thick album labeled *Our Family*. That's a joke. It should be labeled *Our Family: The Abridged Edition*. All that's left where the photos of Mom used to be are the little black corner tabs.

Finally, I hear the scrape of chrome against curb as the Vic backs slowly into the street. I turn around, prepared to wave. But Dez, looking small behind the wheel, never even glances my way.

Dad waves at her taillights, then stands in the road until the car disappears around the corner. He nods to Lonny then walks slowly up the driveway. For a guy who irons everything, Dad looks strangely crumpled.

"Better get going, Dad."

"There was something I wanted to talk to you about…" He stands there, fishing his memory.

"I'm sure we covered it, Dad." I change the subject. "Why'd you pack the album?"

"I read that looking at familiar photographs sometimes helps Alzheimer's patients retain their memories."

"That album sure wouldn't help me retain mine."

The only response from Dad is a frown. We don't talk about Mom. Ever. I just broke the rules—but I'm desperate to keep him from remembering the test.

He lowers the trunk lid and presses until it clicks, then climbs in behind the wheel and adjusts the mirror. "Call me every day, okay? I don't want to run up Nana's phone bill."

"You've got it."

I see my father's eyes reflected as he checks the wing mirrors. "I left Angelica Holland's number on the refrigerator for emergencies. Don't hesitate to use it if you need help. She's expecting you to call."

"I will, Dad." I say it seriously—like there are actual circumstances under which I'd call the assistant principal.

Dad hangs an elbow out the open window. His myopic gray eyes peer into mine. "Keep going on Verbal. The acquisition of a few strategic words could make all the difference next Saturday."

"You forgot the warning about unauthorized parties."

Dad looks confused. "Were you thinking about having one?"

"No, but…I *am* sixteen."

He reaches out and pats my arm. "I'm not worried. I know I can trust you, son."

"Sad but true." I do a short drum roll on the hood, walking beside the car as it backs into the street. "Drive safe, Dad. Don't speed."

"I'm as likely to speed as you are to throw a party," he comments as the car crawls away from the curb.

Sad but true. For a second we trade smiles like the losers we are—or is that just my thinking? Sometimes I forget about his irony deficit.

He taps the horn before putting it into drive—one quick toot so he doesn't disturb the neighbors—and I am home free!

All of a sudden the brake lights fire up. The Nissan shudders. Dad's pale face pops out the window. "The chemistry exam! How did you do?"

"What do you think?" I ask. The smile on my face feels painted on, but Dad doesn't notice. "I aced it." He raises a fist, like I just scored a TD. He's beaming when he takes off.

Lonny flicks a fire-fall of sparks into the street. "Liar," he says.

"It's what he wants to hear." I jam my hands in my pockets and my fingers encounter something hard. "I forgot to give you back your diploma," I say, and I toss the stone to him.

It falls into his palm. "Had more fun getting mine than you are getting yours." He flips the rock into the air a few times before pocketing it. "Where's the old man going?"

"Miami." I slump against his brother's mailbox.

"Your mom at home?"

"What mom?"

"Oh, right," he says. "Don't I know that story…" He smoothly shifts gears. "A few days on your own? Might be your chance to have a little fun."

And I think, *oh yeah, lots-o-fun.* Study, study, and more study—which seems suddenly pointless.

"I'm about to head out myself," he says. "I'm catching the Dog in the morning."

"The what?"

"Greyhound. Gotta put a roof on a friend's house." He rolls his shoulders a couple of times. "Hey, why don't you come along for the weekend? I could use your help. And you *definitely* need a change of scenery."

"I don't know…I think I'd better—"

"You think too much." He drops his cigarette butt on the ground where it joins the growing pile. "You want to come, meet me out here, seven-thirty in the a.m."

I sit at my desk until midnight studying vocabulary. Sometimes when I look up I see Dave Traynor's darkened house across the street, and sometimes I focus on Dad's index card taped to the windowsill. *What is the real question?*

I wish to hell I knew.

4

I sit on the curb at the end of our driveway, backpack between my feet. It's seven-forty and the Traynors' house looks dark. Lonny probably took off already. He's not a by-the-clock kind of guy. I should be relieved. Now I can stay here and study. Big whoop.

But, damn. I had it all worked out. Dad puts most of my tutoring money in the bank for college, but I keep some aside—my secret contingency fund. Even after paying the vet, I have plenty of cash. And thanks to an AT&T calling card purchased when I went to D.C. for the Latin Bowl, Dad would have gotten his nightly call. As for the acquisition of strategic vocabulary, *Word Power* is buried among the T-shirts and socks in my pack.

I stand up and give the pack a savage kick. Normally, it would break my foot, but filled with clothes it rolls a few feet up the driveway. I'm about to kick it again when I hear a shout. "Hey, Fish!" Lonny stands in the door of his brother's house, a khaki duffle bag slung across his back. "You coming along?"

"Sure, why not?"

"Why the hell not," Lonny agrees.

I pick up my scuffed pack and thrust my arms through the straps. Walking back down the driveway, I feel the sun on my face.

"You get permission?" he asks as my stride falls in with his.

"Hell, no."

"Good man." We head toward the Taltran stop to catch a bus to the Greyhound station. When we get to the stop Lonny lights up.

Two smokes later the city bus pulls up with a warm huff. As long as I've lived in Tallahassee, which is my whole life so far, I've never ridden a city bus. Five minutes into my trip with Lonny and things are already different.

I find out where we're going when we buy our tickets: Chiefland, Florida. I'll admit it, I'm disappointed. Chiefland's definitely not exciting—it's not even that far away. Plus, it's going to cost me thirty plus change for the privilege of helping Lonny fix someone's roof. But when I think about sitting at my desk all weekend, I pull the wad of cash out of the flap of my pack. I'm peeling off fives when Lonny says, "Jeez, Fish, don't flash that around in here."

"Why are we buying one-way tickets?" I ask, stuffing the roll of bills back in the pouch.

"It pays to hang loose."

Now that's something I'd like to see on an index card in my room.

Routing tags flapping, we heft our packs and walk over to the waiting area. All seats are full. Sleepers occupy three each. Mouths open, they snore loudly. "Too bad you don't have wheels," observes Lonny, nodding toward a couple guys who look like they should be at the homeless shelter on the next block. "This place is the hall of broken dreams." Dez would appreciate the metaphor—Lonny probably lifted it from a country song.

Nearby, a baby is crying. The girl who holds it rocks back and forth, to comfort it, I assume, but she doesn't seem that interested.

A husk of an old woman runs over my toe with the pink Scooby-Doo travel case she's dragging. I apologize to her—Dad's training. She plows straight ahead, making a beeline for the ladies' room.

Lonny drops his bag on the floor by the wall. "Keep an eye on my stuff, Fish." He goes outside to smoke.

I sit cross-legged on the floor by our bags. There's something square in Lonny's duffle, a box of some kind. I lift the end of the bag and give it a shake. Whatever it is jingles. When I glance up, I'm being watched by two Mexican men who squat on their heels by the door marked Orlando. I nod. One of them shifts the toothpick in his mouth from one corner to the other. They keep staring.

Our fellow travelers look like extras from *Invasion of the Body Snatchers* after the takeover.

It's a relief when the loudspeaker crackles and a voice announces our bus through door three. Lonny jackrabbits back inside and hoists the duffle over a shoulder.

The girl and the crying baby are getting on our bus. Of course. The Scooby-Doo woman emerges from the gaggle waiting by the restrooms and scuffs up the steps behind her. "Put some of this in his bottle," she says, holding out a can of Sprite. "It won't hurt him none. It's caffeine free."

Lonny claims an empty double seat and points me to one across the aisle. He promptly turns his duffle bag into a pillow and crashes.

He ignores a very interesting speech delivered by the bus driver: "There will be no smoking or drinking or drugs. No sex in the seats." Lynelle could use that line on the backseat riders of Number 47. "Any of that stuff goes on in my bus, I'll put you out by the side of the road." He pauses to give that a chance to sink in.

"We'll be making occasional stops where you can visit the restroom or eat. I'll tell you how long you have. Anyone not back on the bus at the designated time will be left behind." Our driver wraps the talk up with an unenthusiastic "Thank you for choosing Greyhound."

"And God bless you too," calls a voice from the back.

Most of the passengers kill the two-and-a-quarter hour ride by going comatose. The baby is quiet, sucking down sugar and bubbles. In the seat in front of me, the Scooby-Doo woman is struggling with a Search-a-Word puzzle. "Parrot...parrot...," she mouths quietly. Between the seats I can easily see the mealy newsprint page she's staring at. "Parrot" and half a dozen other words are painfully obvious. I want to grab the pencil and circle things. "Upper left," I finally mumble.

"So that's where it was hiding!" She circles the word. "You don't happen to see 'rabbit' do you?" I reach over the seat and touch the *R*. We go on like that for a while. She says a word. I find it. She's amazed. But when we finish the whole puzzle in five minutes she closes the book. "My puzzle book has to last me the whole trip," she explains. After that she shows me pictures from her purse: Dave, the son she's going to visit; her grandkids; her husband Mort who passed last winter, "rest his soul."

"How about you?" she asks. "You have pictures?"

All I have is the photo on my driver's license and the only one I'd show it to is a cop. I look like I'm being electrocuted. Besides, she already knows what I look like. Instead, I introduce myself. She snakes a scrawny arm between the seats. "Mrs. Ima Glover," she says. "Pleased to meet you." Her hand reminds me of Nana's. It's splotchy with thin, papery skin. I think briefly of Dad—guilt hammers me—but it passes.

She's telling me about her dog, Skinny, when the bus pulls off the road. The driver bawls, "Perry…Perry. You have ten minutes, people."

The smokers, including Lonny, bail fast. They stand around the bus, sending up an impressive smoke column.

I'm digging a five out of the pack flap for a candy bar when the hand reappears between the seats holding a limp half sandwich. "Cream cheese and jelly. Take it. Save your money. It's hard to come by."

The ten minutes pass. As he climbs back aboard, Lonny looks over at the driver, who is now standing in front of the convenience store holding the soda-slurping baby while the girl talks frantically into the pay phone. Lonny shakes his head. "There's a guy with a cream-filled center." He stretches out on his seat and passes out again. The girl takes the baby back, then hugs the driver. She stays behind; he climbs back on and huffs, "I hope you're all here."

"Glad you could make it," comes that same voice from the back, and we wheel out of the parking lot.

After eating the sandwich I want to wash my hands. I'm about to hit the restroom at the back of the bus, but when I stand, Mrs. Glover says, "I wouldn't go in there, hon. It's always real nasty." I wipe my sticky fingers on the legs of my jeans, sit back down, and cross my arms. The bus sways, and all of a sudden my eyelids are heavy. Must be the soporific effect of cream cheese and jelly.

I don't know how long my head has been tapping against the glass when the driver swings the bus across the center line. My eyes open and we're rolling into the parking lot of Bett's Big T Diner and Truck Stop. The driver brakes and my window is eclipsed by a horse trailer, the words Shady Z Ranch scrawled on its side.

"Chiefland, Chiefland. We'll be here for forty minutes, check your watches, people. I said forty. Feel free to eat lunch, visit the restroom, but be back on the bus in forty or we leave without you."

Lonny sits up and stretches. "Let's go, Fish."

"Have a great time with your son," I tell Mrs. Glover. She totters to her feet and hugs me.

Lonny steers me down the aisle. "Move it, Fish, before she adopts you."

We follow two girls through the diner's swinging doors, all-night riders with blankets around their shoulders. They slide into a booth. Lonny struts up to the counter. He eyes the waitress, but she snatches a couple of menus and strides toward the girls in the booth. "Something to drink to start out with?" she asks them.

I claim a stool but turn my back to the counter and look around. With its wood walls and booths, Bett's is kind of handmade looking. Three cowboys sit at a table in the middle of the room, spurs on their worn boots—probably ranch hands on the Shady Z. Two eat with their hats on; the third's hat hangs over a knee. I had assumed "cowboy" was one of those professions that had ridden off into the sunset, but here's living proof I was wrong. Elbows planted, they lean over their plates, giving their full, silent attention to meatloaf and fried potatoes. One of them glances at me, but his eyes keep traveling. Whatever he sees doesn't match any important shape in the cowboy lexicon.

One of the bus girls drops some change in the jukebox. Guitars twang. *Your cheatin' heart…will tell on you…*

Lonny rests a boot on the bottom rung of the nearest stool and leans across the counter toward the waitress who is getting the girls' coffee. "Hey there, darlin'."

Great. Lonny's hitting on the waitress. She fills two thick

china cups without once looking at him. When she hustles the coffee over to the booth he turns and props his elbows on the counter behind him. "Gotta say, you're lookin' good."

She pulls a pencil from behind her ear to take their orders, but Lonny won't quit. "You been working out, or what? Hey, I'm talking to you, darlin.'"

She walks back to the counter, in short, stiff strides. "Don't you 'darlin' me. Anything between you and me now is strictly business, Lonny Traynor."

Wait—he knows her. They have a history—a bad history. I wonder what the connection is? Small and pale with freckled arms, she's one of those girls you tend to look past. Age-wise she looks about like a college sophomore.

She tears the girls' order off her pad and clips it to a line hanging over the pass-through to the kitchen. "Quit breathing up all the air," she snaps. Lonny just keeps grinning.

He finally swings a leg over the stool and sits. "How about a couple cups of java?" She puts her knuckles on her hips and stares him down. "Come on, me and the kid need a little jump start before we hit the roof."

"You and what kid?" She turns and catches me staring at her. I feel my face flush. "Who's this?"

"This is Fish. You remember him...cousin Larry's oldest?"

The waitress and I both turn toward him like, what?

"Bullshit." She picks up a rag and starts mopping the counter. "Larry don't even *have* a son."

"Sorry, Fish. She never could keep the family straight."

"You're the one I couldn't keep straight!" She flicks his arm with the rag in her hand.

"Calm down, woman, I'm doing an introduction here. Fish, this is Sissy."

She pushes her bangs back with her wrist, studying me warily, then holds out her hand. "Sissy Erle. Pleased to meet you, I guess." Her fingers are cool and damp from the dishrag. Gradually the corners of her mouth turn up. "You look like a nice kid, Fish. Don't let this man rub off on you." I notice that her eyes are a clear, shallow-water blue. She's prettier than I thought.

"You can stop holding hands now," Lonny complains. "I need that coffee sometime today."

She gives my hand a quick squeeze before letting go. "You'll get that coffee when I'm good and ready." But standing on tiptoes she lifts a couple of saucers off a shelf. They land in front of us with a clatter. She fills two cups, deliberately spilling a little of Lonny's. "Oops," she says, looking over at me.

Lonny adds cream, then picks up the glass sugar tower.

Sissy counts, "One Mississippi...two Mississippi...." Sugar pours into the cup for five Mississippis. "Gonna rot your teeth. Seriously, Lonny, are you *ever* gonna grow up?"

The freckles I first noticed on her arms are everywhere, even in the open V of her collar. She blushes as she smooths the collar with her fingers. I take a sudden interest in the pattern on the countertop. "How about you, cousin Fish?" she asks. "What do you take in yours?"

I'm not a frappuccino double latte guy like Raleigh; I don't drink coffee. I'm still trying to figure out what I take when Lonny answers for me. "Same as mine." He dumps five Mississippis of sugar into my cup too. "You know what would go good with this coffee?" He reaches across and swipes a wad of napkins from her apron pocket. "Sandwiches."

She holds up her hands. "Don't start with me. Don't even start! You owe *me*, I don't owe you. It's time you went to work." She fishes keys out of her apron pocket and tosses them at him.

Lonny catches them by the ring and spins them on his finger. "What're you drivin' these days?" he asks.

"The same thing I was drivin' them days. It's parked out back."

Lonny chugs the rest of his coffee. I've barely tasted mine. I take one big swallow as he heads for the door and abandon the rest.

"Hey!" Sissy calls after him.

"Hey what?" he answers, walking backwards a couple of steps.

"You ever gonna ask about Charlie?"

"Oh, yeah." He rests a shoulder against the door frame. "How's Charlie?"

She folds her arms and presses her lips into a single, hard line.

I snag a bus schedule from the rack by the door. "Thinking about an exit strategy?" Lonny asks loudly as I fold the flier and stuff it in a pocket. "I don't blame you, kid. Dealing with Sissy Erle is like being up to your ass in alligators." He pops the swinging door open. After it flaps shut behind us he adds, "But she's cute, ain't she, Fish?"

It doesn't seem safe to go there, but I remember her pale blue eyes and the freckles that disappear into the open neck of her blouse. She is definitely cute.

"It's worse than I remembered," Lonny groans as we come around the end of the diner. The only thing parked out back is a wart-brown car with blistered paint and a bumper sticker that says, *Don't laugh—it's paid for.* "Pile in, Fish, it ain't locked."

Before I can pile in I have to move a box of crackers, a fat green crayon, and an issue of *House Beautiful* that looks like it's done time in a doctor's office.

"Sissy-girl," he mutters as we fishtail down the unpaved road, "it's a miracle you still got an exhaust system."

We kick up a dust cloud for a couple miles before Lonny turns at a leaning mailbox marked Bonita Erle. After weaving between scrub pines and palmettos, the car coasts to a stop in the shade of a massive oak. Lonny crosses his arms on the wheel. "There it is. House Beautiful."

Through leaves and bent limbs I get my first view of a very tall two-story house. Curtainless dormer windows stare from the second story. An ancient VW camper sits on four flats beside the house, returning to the soil. Its carapace is crusted with bumper stickers. "I didn't know you could go somewhere to see the world's biggest ball of string," I say.

"It wasn't all that much to look at," says Lonny. "I mean, it was tall as a man, but big deal, string is string. But she just *had* to see it."

"Wait a minute, wait! Is Sissy the girlfriend you went to the Pacific with?"

"Bingo."

"And we're doing her roof?" My eyes pan up the house. *"That* roof?" It's about two hundred feet in the air and big as a football field.

"That would be the one." He kicks the car door open. "You ask me, she'd do better to let the old place fall in and buy herself a nice double-wide. But this was her granny Bonita's house and Sissy can't let it go. Come on. I'll show ya our little project."

He leads me to a blue tarp that's been covering whatever it's covering for so long that there are pools of mosquito larvae in the sags—microhabitats.

"Grab a corner," he says. As we walk the tarp back, the water splashes against the ground. The stink of mildew almost knocks me over.

Lonny kicks a roll of thick, dark material. "Here's your felt." He nudges one of several paper-wrapped bundles. "And your shingles. This is it, ladies and gentlemen. Sissy Erle's new roof."

"Hope she has good insurance," I say, craning my neck for another look at the roof.

"Sissy don't have squat. That's why we're doing her roof."

"Nice of us." I feel the hairs stand up on the back of my neck. "It looks steep."

"It's got a 6-12 pitch to it. That's nada." At the bottom of the porch steps Lonny rolls over a rock with the toe of his boot. He unlocks the front door with the key underneath, then slips the key in his pocket.

We both walk in, but he stalls just inside the door. "Crap, I hate this place. It feels like a jail."

It feels okay to me. The furniture is dilapidated—Mrs. Z's old couch would be an improvement. The house is run down, but it's clean. The only mess is a pile of romance novels, the kind Desiree calls slut lit, that drift high at one end of the couch.

Lonny points to the staircase. "The sooner we start, the sooner we blow out of here."

Walking the upstairs hall, I look through the open door of a bedroom. Bras and pantyhose are strewn on a rack in front of the window. My glasses jump when Lonny slaps the back of my head. *Whap.* "What was that for?"

"Show some respect, Fish. You never seen ladies' underwear before?"

"Is that what those were?" I rub my head. Without a woman's legs in them, stockings are about as big a turn-on as deflated balloons. Two of the bras were held together with safety pins.

The room at the end of the hall is larger than Sissy's, but it's kind of empty. Two single beds are shoved against opposite walls. In between is a rag rug faded to the color of old newspapers, with plastic soldiers scattered on it.

As he crosses the room, Lonny steps on a stuffed rabbit. He raises the window and climbs out.

Before following him onto the roof, I pick up the rabbit, put it on a bed.

I stand just outside the window, my toes ramming the

fronts of my sneakers. When he said "roof" I should have remembered how much I hate heights. While I stand there, immobile, Lonny strides through patches of sun and shadow, kicking at the corners of shingles. He looks up and catches me playing statue. "Crap, Fish. Please don't tell me you're claustrophobic."

"Afraid of small spaces? No, stuff me in a closet—I'm fine."

"You know what I mean." He saunters to the very edge of the roof. "It's no big deal, see?" And he lifts a foot like he's about to step off. "What do ya say, Fish. Wanna see me fly?"

"That would be highly entertaining," I say, but the truth is he's scaring the bejesus out of me. I take off my glasses and set them carefully on the windowsill, pulling an old trick on myself. When I turn around again—big improvement. The roof within a three-foot radius is real. My own feet are real. Lonny? Not so much. In fact, everything beyond arm's reach is a smear of color. Selectively blind, I stroll to the middle of the roof. Lonny's right—a 6-12 pitch is nada.

"Better than reading a book?" Lonny asks as a fresh breeze flattens my jeans against my legs and a giant scribble of tree bows toward us.

"One for you, one for me." Lonny thrusts the handle of a flat shovel at me.

"Looks like a snow shovel."

"Forget snow. We gotta scrape off the shingles." He rests

the handle of his shovel against his shoulder and knots a red bandanna around his forehead.

"Can't we just nail the new ones on top?" I ask.

"Nope. A roof as old as this, we have to take it down to the plywood. We'll be lucky if we don't have to tear that out too."

This is definitely more than a two-day job. Note to self: peruse the bus schedule.

Lonny spits on his palms and grabs the handle of his shovel. "You watching, Fish?" He wedges the shovel blade between two rows of shingles, gives it a kick to get it started, then pushes. Shingles curl away from the roof. "That's pretty much all there is to it. Rocket science, right?" He slides the shovel to the next spot and gives it a kick. "Whatever you do, don't walk on the loose shingles. It's sort of like stepping on a banana peel."

"Got it." I chock the shovel blade against a row of shingles and give it a kick. When I feel it bite I throw my weight against the handle. The shovel blade snaps the edge of the shingles, then flies out of my hands. All of a sudden, I'm falling up the roof, arms outstretched like Buzz Lightyear.

"Whoa, whoa, whoa!" Lonny snags my belt and holds on as the shovel spins down the roof and goes airborne. To infinity and beyond! There's a sickeningly long pause before we hear it hit the ground.

Lonny releases my belt then hands me his shovel. "Keep working on it." He climbs back through the open window to retrieve the shovel I dropped.

This job will take some getting used to. In order to strip shingles you have to face uphill. I still feel like one wrong move and I'll slide off the roof just like the shovel. I experiment cautiously. I stand with my knees locked. I stand with my knees relaxed. Both ways feel wrong.

Lonny climbs back through the window, shovel in hand. "What're you trying to do, Fish, think them shingles off the roof?"

My first efforts are wimpy, but I quickly discover it takes more force, not less. The trick is to kick the shovel deep under the shingles before pushing. Once you're dug in, it's all push. When my first strip of shingles yawns back from the roof, Lonny says, "Hey, all right! You got it on the run now, kid."

"Nothing to it." I feel pretty good.

For about ten minutes. My legs are strong from running, but this job is mostly upper body. My shoulders start to burn. Pencil pushing hasn't built the right muscles for roof work. I glance over at Lonny to see how he's doing. His bandanna is turning dark. At least he has the decency to sweat.

I let Lonny lug the shingles to the edge of the roof—even without glasses I don't want to get that close to the precipice. He opens his arms and the shingles fall, forming a loose heap on the ground.

I'm surprised at how hard Lonny works. And when he kicks back he does that hard too. I fall into his rhythm. Lonny strips shingles; I strip shingles. Lonny sits and smokes; I stretch out.

It's only when I'm flat on my back that the fear of falling is completely gone and I can totally relax. My shoulders are sore, but the ache hangs in the background, like grocery store music. The smell of warm tar paper fills my nostrils. Brain activity is near zero; thinking got jettisoned with the first armload of shingles. I doze.

I don't notice the warm sun on my face until something blocks it. I open my eyes. Lonny is standing over me. "See what you can scare up in the kitchen, Fish. A couple sandwiches, a couple beers." The word sandwiches wakes up my stomach.

Man, am I hungry.

The bread bag on the table has around half a dozen slices of Hofstra-white in it. But when it comes to things to put between the bread, Sissy's refrigerator is pretty empty. Top shelf: a jug of red punch and a carton of eggs. Second shelf: a couple of slices of turkey lunchmeat, an extra-large jar of grape jelly, a bottle of ketchup. Bottom shelf: a lone bowl of Spaghetti-Os covered with plastic wrap. Two slices of turkey won't make two sandwiches, and I don't want to leave Sissy flat. There's got to be peanut butter around here somewhere to go with all this jelly.

I start opening cupboards. Not that much in there either: chipped plates, cartoon juice glasses, a few pots and pans. A mayonnaise jar that says "tips" on the side holds a few crumpled bills and some quarters, dimes, nickels, even pennies. A jar of Skippy smooth lurks behind the change jar. I take out the peanut butter and jelly and slap together a couple of sandwiches.

There's no beer, only the red punch, and red punch makes you sterile. Seriously. It's not an urban legend. It's been proven in clinical tests—at least if you're a mouse.

Why take a chance? I find a plastic jug and fill it with tap water.

We sit on the roof peak and pass the jug back and forth. "You make a mean PB&J, Fish."

"Yeah, it's okay." I've never tasted a better sandwich. Compared to the sprouted wheat Dad insists on, the white bread is soft and moist; it doesn't fight back. And, as Hofstra proves daily, it has an amazing compression ratio. It starts out fluffy and thick and ends up wafer-thin and glued to the roof of my mouth. I'm prying it off with my tongue when I suddenly remember Dez. I wish I'd gone on not thinking. But the gerbil's in the wheel; the thought is up and running.

By now she's called my house. Instead of getting me she got the gritty silence of the machine followed by my voice: "You have reached the phone of Walt and Fisher Brown. Your call means nothing to us. If compelled to leave a message you may do so after the beep."

At ten feet away I can't see Lonny in detail, but my hearing works fine. "Are you doing what I think you're doing?"

"Depends on what you think I'm doing." The sound, like rain falling on distant leaves, goes on.

I rest on my shovel. "Don't you feel a little exposed?"

Lonny bends his knees, straightening them as he zips. "When you gotta go, you gotta go." He walks back over to his dropped shovel, slides a boot toe under the handle, flips it up, and catches it. It's barely smacked his palm when we hear the purr of tires on sand. "Close one," he says.

I retrieve my glasses. The background snaps into focus as an ancient baby blue Cadillac slides to a stop in the yard. Behind the wheel is a heavy brunette. Sissy's riding shotgun. There's lots of activity in the back seat. I count four heads.

Lonny cocks the shovel handle back against his shoulder and cups his hands around his mouth. "Hel-*lo*, Rhoda!"

The driver sticks an arm out the window and gives Lonny the finger.

"I love you too," he yells.

The rear car door pops open. A boy who looks about five scrambles out, then stops. The three still in the back seat yell, but the kid in the yard stands perfectly still. With the sun on him, his pale skin is translucent, like it's not quite thick enough to hold him in and the world out. His freckles match Sissy's, but his reddish blond hair is Lonny all the way. I look back and forth between them, adding two and two but not believing the answer.

Suddenly, the kid's face lights. When I look over at him Lonny is doing a strange arm signal. His fist, which starts out pulled back against his shoulder, bobs up and down as he extends the arm toward the boy. The move resembles the action of a swimming sperm (made famous in health class videos).

While the boy does the swimming sperm—or whatever it is—back, Sissy climbs out of the car hugging a Styrofoam container. As Sissy slams the car door, Rhoda smacks the horn. "Now hear this, Lonny Traynor! You walk off without finishing that roof and I'll hunt you down and kill you. You got that?" Chuffing up righteous fantails of sand, Rhoda makes a K-turn in the yard and drives away.

Sissy takes the kid's hand. As they walk toward the house, she watches the ground, but the boy's chin lifts higher with each step, his eyes on Lonny.

Feet pound the stairs. "Come *on*, Mom!" The kid's voice is squeaky with excitement.

His face appears at the window. I wave. The face disappears. Sissy sticks a leg through the window and climbs out. She still wears the powder blue uniform and apron, the pantyhose and crepe-soled shoes. Hands on her hips, she surveys the work. "Coming along," she concedes grudgingly, then turns toward the boy, who has a knee on the windowsill. "Stay inside, baby. Daddy'll give you a hug after he cleans hisself up."

I turn toward Lonny.

Lonny shrugs, like how this Daddy-thing happened is a mystery to him. Sissy sees the shrug. "Don't you act all innocent!" She walks right up and stands toe-to-toe with him. Neither one of them pays attention to the face at the window, looking and looking.

"Hey." I go over to the boy and kneel down. "I'm Fish."
I hold out a hand. "I bet you're Charlie. Your daddy talks
about you all the time." We exchange a solemn shake.

"That is just plain disgusting," says Sissy as Lonny smothers
leftover Bett's meatloaf with ketchup. She jerks the bottle out
of his hand and sets it on the table. Her son snatches it up
and tries to empty it over his own plate.

"What's goin' on, Charlie? Monkey-see, monkey-do?"
She takes it away from him and carries it to the refrigerator.

At home Dad would ask about my day, I'd ask about his;
nothing momentous, but we'd talk. Here, the only sound is
fork music. Sissy cradles her chin in one hand and picks at
the food on her plate. Lonny eats the same way he smokes,
like a man on a mission.

Lonny's cleaned up, but he hasn't hugged Charlie yet.
Watching Charlie laser-beam him with his eyes, I want to
kick Lonny under the table. The kid is drowning in his chair,
waiting for his father to notice him.

I look at the desolate kid, then back at Lonny. Then, with
my fork, I start rearranging the food that's left on my plate.
When things are beginning to shape up, I bump Charlie's leg
with my knee.

His eyes veer away from Lonny and toward the evolving
face of Dinner Man. French fry eyebrows float above peas
that double as squinty eyeballs—resources are limited. I
begin to line up carrot slices for the mouth.

The kid doesn't smile, but he's watching. Then, all of a sudden, he starts to help. He plops down a couple of meat-loaf ears, a french fry mustache. Having barely touched his dinner, he has a full plate of materials to choose from.

"Dinner Man thanks you," I whisper, expecting Sissy to yell at us.

But when I glance over at Sissy, she is half smiling. "You have a way with kids, Fish."

"That's 'cause he *is* a kid." Lonny drops his paper napkin on the table. "Hey, Charlie. I brought you something."

"For really?" Charlie breathes.

"Look in my duffle bag. Quick now, before it gets away."

Charlie runs to the next room. He comes back hugging a long box.

"An Erector set!" I whoop. "I love those things."

Sissy taps a fingernail on the end of the box. "It says eight years and up, Lonny. Couldn't you find him something he could actually *play* with?"

Lonny tips his chair up on two legs and reaches for the cup of toothpicks on the stove. "Charlie's a smart kid, aren't you, Charlie? And you heard Fish, these things are cool."

"But he's way too young for an Erector set," Sissy says. "How'd you pick it out anyway?"

"A guy owed me some money, he couldn't come up with all of it, so he gave me the toy."

"So you didn't choose it. I should have known."

Lonny leans across the table. "Well ex-*cuse* me for trying." He jerks the box out of Charlie's arms and hurls it through the door to the living room. Metal pieces clank as it skids across the floor.

Charlie's mouth is open. I can tell that he wants to cry, and that he's afraid to. I stare into my lap. Mom and Dad never threw things; they never yelled. They fought with words and, more often, they fought with silence. Different kitchen, different parents, different weapons, but it's like I'm back there.

"What's for dessert?" Lonny asks. When I look up he's selecting a toothpick like nothing happened.

"Dessert?" Sissy puts her arms around Charlie. "You scare your kid half to death and ask for dessert?"

"Come on, girl, quit babying him. The kid's fine. Aren't ya, Charlie?"

"No he's not. Tell him, Charlie!"

They're pulling on the kid like a wishbone. But Charlie won't look at either one of them. His neck is a broken stem. He won't lift his eyes from the floor.

I'm breathing hard. I have to get out of the room. "Mind if I make a call?" I ask. I snake the phone card out of my pocket and hold it out, so Sissy doesn't think I'm going to run up her bill.

She waves a hand. "Phone's in by the TV."

As I walk out of the kitchen Lonny says, "What do you say, Charlie? Bet I can throw an Erector set farther than anybody else's daddy. You think I'd win the gold medal?" There's a pause, then Charlie's shaky laugh. "Come on over here," Lonny coaxes. "Seems like you owe me a hug."

"You jerk!" says Sissy. I hear the sound of a slap. But it's a friendly "you jerk" and a playful slap. Maybe this is the way it is with them. They play and they fight. Sometimes they keep their claws in, sometimes they don't. Does either one of them think about Charlie?

I carry the cordless up the stairs. Sitting on the top step, I dial the string of numbers on the calling card—a sequence long enough to launch World War III—before finally getting to the number at Nana's house.

By now Nana's in her new digs, but Dad'll be staying at the old house until the guys from Goodwill pick up the furniture and he locks the door for the last time.

It rings three times before he picks up. "Hello?"

"Hey, Dad."

"Fisher..." I hear the smile in his voice; it's like the guy who used to fight with Mom was someone else. "How was your Saturday, son? I hope you didn't study too much."

"No, not too much."

"Did you do okay with the cooking?"

"Didn't burn the house down, blow a breaker, or anything." Dad thinks I'm ready for Yale—but not quite up to feeding myself.

"Listen, Fisher, get some rest this week, hit vocabulary hard, but don't study all the time. You don't want to peak too soon."

"I got it, Dad. Stay sub-peak until Saturday. How's Nana?"

Dad sighs. "Confused. Ocean Zephyr is a lovely place, but she doesn't have any idea where she is. Sometimes she thinks she's in high school. Sometimes she thinks I'm Grand-dad."

"That's weird."

"Tell me about it!"

By keeping things focused on Nana I get out of the conversation without lying, at least technically. After I hang up I feel bad. I didn't lie, but I left out a lot. It's like I failed to mention I had a girl in my room.

Bad analogy. When have I ever had a girl in my room? Except Dez, who doesn't count.

But I need this break. I deserve this break. And everything is fine. So, no big deal.

I put the phone on the coffee table and catch sight of the corner of the Erector set. I pick up the box. Did the guy who owed Lonny steal it from his own kid? If so, the kid didn't get to play with it. The box is virgin—never been opened. I turn it over in my hands. With a motor and a complete set of ropes and pulleys, it's pretty deluxe. Sweet.

"Hey, Fish!" Lonny bellows from the kitchen. "Move it. Your ice cream's melting."

I lean the box against the wall.

My Choco-Berry Crunch sits in a purpley-brown puddle. Charlie wilts over his own melting ice cream. Lonny and Sissy smoke. They're in the silent phase. My parents went there a lot. It seems like it would be better than the yelling, but it's not. Silence cuts a kid out of the loop. Under that silence anything could be happening.

"Hey, Charlie," I whisper. "You want to build something with the Erector set?"

Charlie sits up straight. "Something like what?"

"Something like whatever you want."

"You'd help? For really?"

Charlie stares at his dad, but Lonny doesn't offer to help us, he just tells Charlie to finish his ice cream first. Charlie shovels it in fast.

"You act like no one ever plays with you!" Sissy says. "We play together all the time: store, and bunny family, and—"

"Mom…" He squirms away as she brushes his bangs out of his eyes. "That's baby stuff. This is grown up."

She pats his cheek. "Of course it is."

The spoon clangs into Charlie's bowl. "Come on, Fish! Race ya!" I let him win.

"Charlie," I say as I break the seal on the package, "I am about to introduce you to a whole new world." I lift the lid and turn the box over.

Charlie's eyes saucer as the metal sections spill out.

"And look at this." I hold up a small plastic bag. "We've got pulleys and everything. We can build a working crane." We go down on our stomachs.

I show him how to use the Allen wrench, then wait to see if he can do it—he *is* kind of young.

But Charlie's careful, and he's persistent. He tries until he gets it. He works steadily, except when he stops to listen to the adults in the kitchen. His shoulders relax when they laugh. When one of their voices spikes dangerously, no matter how engrossed he is, he turns stiffly toward the kitchen.

"Mommy! Daddy! Come see what Fish and I built!" Charlie cranks the crane up and down, wild with enthusiasm.

In the kitchen Sissy says something about "your son." Chairs scrape.

Sissy makes a big fuss about our crane. Lonny says, "Looks good." They act enthusiastic the way adults do when a thing that has a kid really jazzed doesn't mean much to them. They don't notice the way the shine goes out of Charlie's eyes.

"It's the best," I tell him quietly. "It's the bomb, it's cool!"

"It's the cherry on top!" he whispers back.

The crane makes a little jingling sound as Charlie plays with it. Lonny watches TV. Sissy sits at the opposite end of the couch from Lonny, hugging a stuffed dog that was on the floor. At eight she says, "Charlie, it's bedtime, honey. Scoot upstairs and put on your pj's. I'll be there in five minutes to hear prayers."

"Mom?" He stands in front of her and stares at the stuffed dog in her arms.

"Sorry." She hands the toy to him. "I forgot it's Rudy's bedtime too."

Then, in a lay-down-the-law voice she announces, "Now, about sleeping arrangements. There's the couch and there's the spare bed in Charlie's room. You two work it out."

"I got dibs on the couch," says Lonny. "Let the kids sleep together."

Charlie's lip begins to quiver. I hold out a hand. "Hey. Slap me five, roommate!"

I lug my pack up to his room. Between helping him pull his turtleneck over his head and a string of introductions to the stuffed animals on the beds, I'm still there when Sissy comes up to hear prayers. You don't walk out on God, so I stay, sitting on the edge of Charlie's bed.

Charlie does the list, like I used to: "Bless Mommy and Daddy, and Grandma and Grandpa, Uncle Silas and Aunt Betty, Humpy and George and Rudy…" His list goes on and on. After a while, the names seem familiar….

"Honey," says Sissy, "God's awful busy to be blessing stuffed animals."

"God likes stuffed animals!" Charlie is silent, then, "Read me a story."

"Not tonight, sugar. Daddy and me have to talk."

Charlie begins to cry. He's not throwing a scene; I can barely hear him, but his shoulders shake. "Wait!" I say. "Did I tell you about the roommate rule?"

Charlie snuffs. "What rule?"

"As your new roommate I have to read you a story."

"Good night, boys." Sissy kisses the top of Charlie's head and pats mine. She moves like a cat, silently across the room, out the door and down the stairs.

"So, where are the books?" Charlie shows me the shelf above his bed. On it is a strange combination of books about fossils and a mess of Dr. Seuss. It looks like the collection I used to have.

Charlie picks *The Cat in the Hat*. Fortuitous! I happen to know this one by heart. Mom and I read it a zillion times. "Hey, want to see me read with my eyes closed?" Charlie thinks it's some kind of a trick. Before I can start he ties his sweatshirt around my eyes. It has a funky stale-kid kind of smell.

In the dark inside my own head I see the first page. "'The sun did not shine. It was too wet to play. So we sat in the house all that cold, cold, wet day.'"

Charlie begins to chant along, like I did with Mom. He must know it by heart too. "'I know it is wet. And the sun is not sunny. But we can have lots of good fun that is funny.'" Reciting together we sound like chanters in some weird religious ceremony.

The fish stands up on his tail and scolds the cat. I don't just remember the words, but the pictures, too.

"That's you!" says Charlie. "The fish!"

But the fish doesn't faze the Cat. "It's fun to have fun but you have to know how," the Cat responds. The fish knows the rules, but the Cat has all the fun.

Charlie giggles when the Cat plays the game "Up-up-up with the fish!"

If I draw a blank I let Charlie say the first couple of words, cuing me. We finish the book together. "'What would *you* do if your mother asked *you?*'"

Then Charlie wants me to read *The Grinch Who Stole Christmas* with my eyes closed, but I don't know that one by heart. I tell him the roommate rule only allows one story. I turn on the night-light. Even with the light on, Charlie makes me leave the door open.

I stop at the head of the stairs and listen for voices from the living room. There aren't any. Afraid I might walk in on something, I sit cross-legged on the top step. The SAT prep book is in my pack. I could cram in a word or two for Dad, but after a day on the roof I'm whipped.

Downstairs, Sissy giggles. If Charlie is listening, he probably hopes that, just maybe, everything will work out this time. Hope is hard to kill.

5

eferential…reverential," I whisper. "Referential, from refer. Reverential, from reverent."

It's five-seventeen—I'm definitely the only one in this house with any conscious brain function. Charlie and Sissy are still asleep upstairs; Lonny's on the couch snoring louder than God. It's so cold in this kitchen, my hands are tucked in my pits.

I got up before the alarm would have gone off at home because I had this dream. It featured Raleigh tearing pages out of the dictionary and eating them. He didn't say a word. He just looked up at me, smirked, and went right on ingesting the *R*s.

That's why I'm studying before he—or even the sun—has thought about rising. What little light falls on the open vocabulary book comes from the small fluorescent bulb over the stove.

I pull a hand out of my armpit to flip the page, and I feel a twinge in my shoulder. As an experiment, I lift my arm over my head. Oh yeah, another day on the roof is going to kill me.

"Redoubtable…commanding respect." Re-*doubt*-able? When did doubt become part of respect? Don't analyze, memorize—cramming is no time to mess with etymology.

Tired of the *R*s, I flop the book open to a new place. "Wanton…sexually loose or unrestrained. Wanton."

I jump six and a half feet when fingers trail across my shoulder. As if materializing out of nowhere, Sissy is suddenly there in a thin cotton nightgown and a fuzzy blue sweater. "I didn't hear you come down the stairs," I gasp.

"Too busy talking to yourself, I guess."

"I *have* to. I can't hear myself think over Lonny's snoring." I watch her lean across the counter to plug in a small space heater.

"He snores something fierce," she agrees. Turning away, she goes up on her toes to open a cupboard. The two skinny braids that hang down her back swing. Mom used to braid her hair for bed too—I'd forgotten.

Sissy turns around hugging a red coffee can. Mom vanishes. "What're you doing up so early?"

"Studying for SATs."

"What are they?" She sets the coffee can on the table.

"Scholastic Aptitude Tests? You take them to get into college."

"Wouldn't know." She pops the plastic lid. "I got married instead."

"To Lonny? Of course to Lonny." Typical, I'm babbling.

"I wish I could give that stupid girl a good talk-to," she

says. "I'd tell her, cross your legs, stay in school. I just listened to Lonny—but it wasn't like I had anyone else giving me good advice."

I almost tell her about Dad. She should know there's such a thing as too much good advice.

"Why are you looking at me like that, Fish?"

"Like what?"

"Like you don't think I'm college material?"

"I'm not! I just have this cynical face." I glance down at the page. When I look up again, I'm Dad. "You know, it's never too late to get an education."

It's profound and true, but she blows it off. "All it takes is two things I don't have: time and money." She measures coffee grounds, then drops the scoop back in the can. "I barely stay one step ahead of the next bill. I'm on my own here. I can't count on him." She nods toward the sound of snoring, then lowers her voice. "I'm having him do the roof because it's better than nothing, which is what he's been sending us lately."

"But with an education you wouldn't need him," I whisper back. "Do one class at a time." For a second I feel what Dad must feel when he steers a kid right, because she holds her breath and looks like she's considering it.

Then she lets her breath out. "I can't, Fish. Some days I'm so tired it's all I can do to put one foot in front of the other. You're too young to know about that."

"No, I'm not! I get tired." I flash on Dad's cards taped all over my room—sometimes all I have to do is read them and I'm exhausted. Then I think of her on her feet all day at Bett's. That's a higher magnitude of tired.

97

"What are you studying anyway?" As she tries to read over my shoulder, the end of one braid brushes my neck.

"Words," I squeak—Hofstra and I call it "the cartoon voice." I thought I was done with it years ago.

"That's what they test you on, words? I know lots of words. Wanton," she reads. "Those're the little noodle things in Chinese soup, right?"

"That's right," I say. "Chinese noodles." If someone at Leon said that, they would never live it down—it would be yearbook material. But I keep my face straight. I don't laugh at her.

She tosses a braid over her shoulder. "This test doesn't sound very hard."

"There are other things too. Reading comprehension, sentence completion, analogies."

"Analogies…" I can tell she doesn't know what an analogy is but doesn't want to look stupid.

"You remember analogies. That's when you find something similar between two things that are otherwise different."

She folds her arms, as if she's protecting herself.

"Maybe if I give you an example." I scan for inspiration and see the coffeemaker. "Okay, the analogy might go like this: coffee is to cup as water is to…. Then they give you choices like bathtub, soap, fountain, chocolate pudding— you look for the word that would make the two pairs alike."

She brightens. "It's fountain, right?"

I tug on my ear. "Actually, I think they'd be looking for 'coffee is to cup as water is to bathtub'. You know, the cup holds coffee…and the bathtub holds water?"

Her face falls. "It's no big deal," I say quickly, wishing I'd never brought it up. "They're going to drop analogies from the test next year anyway."

"I don't see what's wrong with 'fountain.' You drink coffee from a cup; you drink water from a fountain. Seems like to get the answer right you have to think just like the guy who made up the test."

She steps out of the kitchen and yells, "Charlie? Ten minutes, sweetie! Your clothes are on top of the hamper."

Wait! Is that what I'm learning, how to think like the guy who made up the test? Wish I could run this by Hofstra and Raleigh. Are we being programmed?

"Lonny?" I hear her pad over to the couch. "You need to get up on that roof." The snoring goes on. "You have until the eggs are ready," she warns. Back in the kitchen, she takes a pot out of the cupboard and sets it on the stove. "Grits and eggs okay?" she asks me.

"Grits and eggs would be outstanding."

Water gurgles through the coffeemaker. The pan of grits belches on the stove. Even if someone cooked breakfast at my house, grits would never happen. Too many simple carbs for Dad. Personally, I like simple carbs.

Sissy props the refrigerator door open with a hip and reaches for the egg carton. In the refrigerator light I can see the shape of her legs through her gown. I shift my eyes to the carton in her hand. "Eggs," I say, "definitely a controlled substance at my house." Covering the fact I was looking at her legs, I've turned into Nerdman. "They're bad for your cholesterol." Once Nerdman opens his mouth it's hard to shut him up. "Actually, the latest data says that eggs in moderation are okay, but try changing my dad's mind."

"Eggs are cheap." She cracks eight into a blue china bowl. As she scrambles them she sings under her breath. "Your cheatin' heart...will make you weep. You'll cry and cry, and try to sleep...."

I hold my hands out to the space heater and listen.

"But slee-eep won't come...the whole night through. Your cheatin' heart...will tell on you."

"This is nice."

She turns, spatula in hand. "What is?"

"You know...all of this. At home I eat breakfast alone."

"Where are your folks?"

"Dad goes to work early. My mom left before dinner one night when I was in sixth grade. I haven't seen her since."

A little late I realize I may have just blown the "Cousin Larry" cover, but she really *doesn't* know Lonny's family. She never even questions it. All she says is, "How can a parent do that?"

I want to say, *ask Lonny*.

Lonny's still snoring when Charlie wanders in looking dopey and dazed.

"Come'ere, roommate, let me check you out." I tug the label sticking out under his chin. "Is this your handle?"

"I got my shirt backwards," the boy says soberly. He squirms his arms back inside. The fabric twists until the sleeves line up with his shoulders again. His hands pop out. All of a sudden, his eyes light up. "Hey, wanna do Erectors?"

Sissy carries the pan of eggs to the table. "You can play Erectors tonight, mister. Right now you have to eat breakfast. But first, go in there and wake your daddy up." Sissy scrapes the eggs onto four plates. When she glances at him again, Charlie's standing in the doorway, staring toward the couch where Lonny is sawing wood. "Go on, sweetie, wake the man up."

He takes a step and looks back over his shoulder.

"Feeling shy, baby?" She sets the pan in the sink, runs a little water into it. "Eat your eggs." And she goes to wake the man up herself.

Charlie climbs into the chair next to mine and picks up his fork.

"Hey, Charlie. Does his snoring sound weird to you?" I ask quietly.

The boy cocks his head toward the other room. "I think he's fake snoring."

"Lonny," Sissy's voice is soft. "Lonny?" The bogus snoring continues. "Lonny," she snaps. "I cooked your eggs, I made your coffee…get your lazy butt out of—" She lets out a scream.

"Mommy!" Charlie knocks his chair over and runs. I'm right behind him.

"Cut that out, cut that out!" Sissy squeals. Lonny has his arms around her ribs.

Charlie jumps up on the couch and throws himself on Lonny's back.

"Quit tickling, you'll make me pee myself!" Sissy's knees buckle and she slides to the floor laughing.

Lonny reaches over his shoulder and peels Charlie off. "Back up, Killer. Your mom and me were just having a little fun."

Sissy scrambles to her feet and straightens her nightgown. "Your breakfast is getting cold." She stalks back to the kitchen.

Lonny throws off the afghan that covers his legs. He's wearing nothing but the tattoo—definitely more of Lonny than I need to see. He steps bare-ass into his jeans, then swings around and points a finger at Charlie. "Your mother is the most ticklish woman in the world."

Charlie holds his ground. "Nuh-uh. Not in the world."

"Yes-huh. I checked."

"Quit talking crap," Sissy calls from the kitchen. "Charlie, get on in here and eat quick. Mommy's got to get dressed and go." She comes out of the kitchen with a full coffee mug in her hand. I watch her bare legs as she climbs the stairs.

Lonny whaps the back of my head again. "Don't even think about it, Snowflake."

"If you keep doing that, I won't be able to think."

"I didn't hit the part you were thinkin' with."

Lonny smothers his eggs with ketchup, then holds the bottle out to Charlie. "How about it, Charlie? Dragon lady's in the shower. You want ketchup like your old man?"

Charlie turns to me. "You like ketchup on your eggs, Fish?"

"No, I take mine straight."

Charlie shakes his head at Lonny. "No, I take mine straight, like Fish."

Lonny stares at me over the kid's head. "Looks like you're winning hearts and minds all over the place."

"Eat your eggs like me, Charlie," I say quickly. "But be strong like your old man, okay?"

"Okay," says Charlie. "I'm pretty strong already." He holds up one scrawny arm and makes a fist. "Feel the muscle." We both feel the muscle and say what a good muscle it is. Lonny's smile returns, but I don't completely trust it. I've seen the dark side take him over a couple of times now. If it wasn't over so fast it would be scary.

Sissy hustles into the kitchen, twisting her damp hair into a bun. "Let's go, Charlie." She grabs her son's chin and wipes his face with a wet paper towel. "Would ya hold still?" He should appreciate the fact that she wet the towel under the tap. Mom always used spit. "I got the breakfast-lunch shift today, plus we got an extra girl. We'll be home early, so I can help," she says, looking from me to Lonny. "You guys work hard 'til then, okay?"

"Why can't I stay here with Fish...?" Charlie begs.

"Come on, Charlie. Fish doesn't have time to play." She gives his butt a light swat. "Miss Rhoda's waitin' on you."

Lonny's chair creaks as he turns to watch her hustle Charlie out of the house. "What?" he calls after her. "No goodbye kiss?" The door closes behind her.

"How long have you two been divorced?" I ask, putting a few finishing touches on Charlie's scrambled egg face.

"Can't get divorced if you never got married." He tosses his fork at the sink.

"But Sissy said—"

"Sissy says a lot of things."

I don't challenge him, but I believe Sissy. Lonny is what Dez calls an unreliable narrator. He tells his story his own way; that doesn't mean it's true. "Quit playing with that food," he says. "We got work to do."

"Sure thing, but don't forget. Tonight I'm out of here."

"Take it easy, Fish. Let tonight take care of tonight." He grins and gives me a friendly shove toward the stairs. "Come on. Daylight's wasting."

I leave the glasses on the windowsill and step out onto the roof. I fall into the posture I learned yesterday by watching Lonny: keep the knees loose, bend forward a little. Today the wind is gusty, and strong enough to push me around. The conspiracy between gravity and wind is going to make things harder, but I feel exhilarated, like I'm living right up at the surface of my skin. I'd never tell Lonny but I'm kind of enjoying this. Lonny takes a long deep breath and gazes out over the trees; maybe he feels it too. "Hoo-wee!" he yelps. "It's colder'n a witch's tit up here."

In half an hour the cold air is feeling pretty good. Roofing is sweaty work. After an hour I toss my sweater behind the chimney—Lonny sheds his T-shirt. If my muscles rippled like his, I'd go down to skin too.

By ten we're ripping the last few shingles off this side of the roof. Lonny watches me kick my shovel. "Take the shirt off. You're sweating like a pig."

When I don't do it he looks over his right shoulder, then his left. "I don't see any babes up here. Nobody's gonna see your chest."

Except you, I think.

But I'm hot. Even though I know a day and a half of heavy labor hasn't changed my bald, pasty, slightly caved-in chest, I reach over my head and grab the neck of my T-shirt. As I peel the shirt off, a chill wind hits my damp chest. My nipples get hard and goose bumpy. I keep my back to Lonny as much as I can—comparisons are inevitable. But after a while I forget about it. Sun and wind feel good on bare skin, and Lonny never comments.

By the time we get down to the boards under the shingles— the layer that Lonny calls the sheathing—I'm practically groaning. Blisters the size of Vesuvius have erupted on both palms.

While Lonny walks the roof, inspecting it, I stretch out, following him with my eyes, the only body part that doesn't hurt. Sometimes he puts his weight on one foot and bounces, to see if the old sheathing is sound. Sometimes he drops to his knees and checks seams. Shuttling back and forth across the roof, he dances in and out of focus.

As my eyes close, a word fragment floats across my brain: *bene-*. It's a root word meaning *good* or *well*. Benefit, beneficent, benediction, benefactor, beneficial, benevolent. The words rock me like small waves and I start to drift off.

"Looks like we got lucky, Fish. Not too much rot." I open my eyes and Lonny's standing over me eclipsing the sun, his edges on fire. "Now comes the heavy lifting."

I sit up with a groan. "You're kidding."

He drops to his heels and lights a cigarette. "Remember that stuff down there?" He jabs the cigarette toward the boxes and rolls of felt, the crumpled tarp. "We have to get what's down there up here."

"Like, carry it?"

"Unless you got a way to beam it up."

I close my eyes. "I'll work on it." But he pops me on the arm and tells me to hustle.

We have to hunt for the ladder. I finally spot it, leaned against the trunk of the live oak. "Maybe Charlie climbs up and sits in that V up there," I say.

"Doubt it. He's kind of chicken shit."

"Charlie's tougher than you think."

"Huh!" he grunts. He puts an arm between the rungs. Scuffed by countless shoes, the rungs look frayed. The whole ladder seems rickety and rotten. As he carries it over to the house I think, I am *not* going up that thing. I wonder how I can say that to Lonny without sounding like total chicken shit.

When the ladder's in place Lonny and I go back and survey the supplies. Yesterday it was just a pile of stuff. Today it's a *heavy* pile of stuff. Lonny drops to one knee, tips a roll of felt back against a shoulder, and lifts. "Beam us up a couple bundles of shingles, okay?"

I force my hands under the first bundle and try to ignore the sensations my fingers are reporting. The paper that wraps the shingles is as slick and cool as school paste. When I try to lift, nothing happens.

"Save your back. Use your legs," Lonny shouts as he grabs a rung of the ladder with his free hand. "That's ninety pounds of dead weight."

I crunch my thigh muscles and lift. The bundle comes up with a glutinous sucking sound. Adrenaline surges. Look at the geek, lifting ninety pounds!

Then I happen to glance down. It's like something out of a Japanese horror flick. The spot where the shingles sat is crawling with pill bugs and millipedes and eyeless white grubs. I open my arms and the bundle of shingles hits the ground with a *whomp*. Shingles tear through the paper wrapping and slide. I've inadvertently dropped the bomb on arthropod city.

Lonny, who has just set the felt on the roof, yells, "Smooth move, Snowflake."

"These aren't shingles! They're habitats!" I object as he comes back down the ladder.

Grinning, Lonny collects a bundle of long metal strips. "Welcome to biology class."

"I try to stay away from life forms whose survival strategy

is to hole up in the dark and mutate, okay?" Trying not to think about what I'm touching, I gather the shingles and lift. Hugging them to my bare chest, I stagger to the ladder, then stop to watch Lonny scrabble up ahead of me. With each step the ladder bends toward the house.

Forget it. No way am I climbing up that thing.

I carry my load through the house, sprinkling a trail of grubs along the way. Overhead Lonny begins to hammer.

I set my load on Charlie's windowsill and brush the black grit off my chest. Lonny is kneeling right at the edge of the roof, nailing a metal strip. One small slip, even a sneeze, could send him over. I don't want to get roped into that job, so I go back for more grubs and shingles.

By the time I deliver the second load, Lonny is standing on the felt, kicking the roll across the roof, laying down the first course. "Nothing to it," he says, slapping a box knife into my hand. He needs to install flashing around the dormer windows—a skilled job.

I'm left with the grunt work, but I don't mind. The brain is in neutral. Despite strains and blisters, the body is enjoying being in charge.

Kneeling at opposite edges of the roof, we each hold one end of a chalky string. "Pull 'er tight," says Lonny, then he plucks the taut string. Just as he lets it go with a snap, marking the dusty line on the felt where we'll place the first row of shingles, Sissy's car comes swamping though the loose sand. The car still in the middle of its death rattle, Charlie bails out of the backseat. "Hey, Fish! Let's do Erectors!"

"I can't," I shout as he dashes across the yard. "I'm playing with Lonny right now."

From inside the house comes the sound of running feet. Charlie's face appears at the window, his eyes on me. "Come on, Fish. Just for ten minutes?"

"Hey, Charlie," Lonny says, redirecting his attention. "Can you give your mom a message?" Charlie nods once. "Say, 'Mother, dearest darling, the two handsome hunks on the roof could use a couple sandwiches.' You got that?"

Charlie parrots it back verbatim, then turns stiffly and hurries away.

Lonny shows me how to nail a strip of shingles, then tosses me the hammer. "It's all yours," he says. I hit my thumb twice and the nails go in crooked, but I think, hey, *close enough*. Like he said, it's not rocket science. But Lonny takes one look at my work and says, "Pull 'em out and do it again."

"No one'll know! The next row will cover them."

"Think about it, Einstein. Unless the nails are flush, they poke holes in the shingles that go over them. Then the roof leaks."

I grab a nail head with the hammer's claw and rock it back and forth, squealing it out of the wood. This isn't that different from the chemistry exam. Close isn't good enough. I guess everything has standards.

I hold the new nail and give it a light tap to get it started. It goes in straight; the next one doesn't. I pull it back out. I'm

109

slick with sweat when I finish the first strip of shingles, but when I run a hand over the nail heads I barely feel a thing. It's too bad I only have a few more hours before I get on the bus. I could get good at this.

"Doesn't seem like that 'mother dearest darling' thing worked, does it?" Lonny says, resting his knuckles on his hips. "My backbone and my bellybutton are shaking hands. I say we borrow her car, go to Chiefland, and get us some grub. She leaves the keys in it."

"Not when you're around," says a voice from Charlie's room, and a pair of arms comes through the window holding a tray loaded with sandwiches, beer, and a hammer.

As I crouch to take the tray from Sissy I notice that curly strands of hair have escaped from the bun that was tight and smooth when she left for work this morning. "Hey," she says softly, the skin around her eyes crinkling in a smile.

"Hey," I repeat, suddenly aware of my bare chest. My face glows with heat. "Got it," I say. I take the heavy tray out of her hands and stand up fast.

Lonny saunters into my spot. Reaching through the window, he grabs her hands. "Can't stay away from the handsome hunks, huh?"

"I'm here to work, period. The sooner the job gets done, the sooner you go back to wherever." But after he lifts her out onto the roof they stand inches apart, and neither one of them steps away. Maybe neither one wants to back down, but it feels like something else.

When Lonny finally lets go of her hands, he runs a knuckle up the inside of her arm. Creeps me out. I don't know what he's trying to do; maybe I don't want to know, but I wish he'd cut it out. "Sandwich, Lonny?" I ask loudly.

He helps himself. The tension disappears—if it was ever there. Dez says I misinterpret life's little signals. She calls me head smart and gut clueless. I might have imagined the whole thing.

I distribute the rest of the sandwiches and toss the tray back into Charlie's room. Charlie is allowed to sit on the windowsill as long as he keeps one leg inside the room. I sit near him, my back against the window frame.

Lonny lies on his side, propped on an elbow. Sissy steps down the roof, putting a good eight feet between them. "Hey, Fish!" Lonny holds up a can of beer and waggles it. "You want?"

Warning signals flash. Don't drink and drive, don't drink and roof. What the hell. I crab-crawl until my fingers touch the can. The icy cold soothes my blisters.

When I get back to the window I pull the tab. This isn't a total first. Sometimes Hofstra and I liberate a few when his parents are out. They don't seem to notice. There are always plenty of beers in their fridge. I've seen Hofstra barfing-drunk on more than one occasion; he can't do anything in moderation. I always stop at one. Hofstra's folks might be oblivious; Dad would definitely notice.

Besides, the taste is real bad—except today. Maybe you have to sweat before beer tastes good. I'm taking a good long swig when Charlie asks, "Want to see my prehistoric mammoth tooth?" Without waiting for an answer, he slides off the windowsill and back into his room.

I hear him rummaging around, then, "Hold out your hand." He thrusts a closed fist at me through the window and drops something cool and heavy in my palm.

"Hey, wow." I turn the fossil over in my fingers. Its surface is corrugated. It looks like a segmented worm morphed into stone, but I used to collect too, so I know. "This really *is* a mammoth tooth."

"A juvenile. Adults had much bigger ones. I found it in Otter Springs." Charlie gets the Golden Guide book on fossils and shows me a picture. "It's a molar, see?" He points to the word, *molar*.

"You're smart, Charlie, you know that?"

His bangs fall over his eyes as he ducks his head, embarrassed by the compliment. What he doesn't understand is, it's not that great a compliment. I know because it's the one I get all the time. Being smart puts you in a box, like being a jock puts you in a box. It won't matter to Charlie for a while, so I don't tell him the really bad news: They put all the hot girls in the box marked "jock."

"Fish?" Lonny says. I glance at him and wonder, how did he get over there? He's sitting inches from Sissy. "Start stripping the other side of the roof. You're good with the shovel. Sissy'll nail shingles."

"I think I've done my share of shovel work." I get it. He just wants me out of the way. I stand up slowly, wondering what Sissy wants.

"Then maybe you'd like to shingle the dormers." Lonny's

not really offering me the job. Given the angles involved, shingling a dormer is skill work.

I glance at my watch and realize I'm out of here in two hours and eleven minutes. What can I change in two hours and eleven minutes?

"Okay, master," I grunt. "Mongo *loves* shoveling shingles." I pick up the flat shovel and a second beer. Brew in hand, I ape over to the other side of the roof. I toss the shovel down, sit, and pull the tab. If he's over there hitting on Sissy, I don't feel any need to rush.

I'm swallowing when I hear *tap, tap, tap.* The pattern repeats four times. It takes four nails to attach a strip of shingles. There's a pause—then it happens again. Sissy's working, not flirting.

A second hammer kicks in. "Okay, okay." I pick up my shovel and stand. Bubbles break against the inside of my skull. Interesting sensation. I take another pull on the beer, then set the can down carefully.

I jam the shovel blade under a row of shingles and rip. Maybe it's the beer. Maybe I'm getting stronger. I tear into the shingles, big-time, clearing swaths. When the sweat starts to pour, I lean over and snag the beer. Barely cool, the brew tastes sweeter and not as good. But what the hell. It's not going to get any colder. I throw my head back and empty the can.

When I pick up the shovel again I knock the can over with my foot. It rolls down the roof. I wave as it plunges over the edge. Since I can actually see it I must have my glasses on. I put a hand to my face, and yup, there they are. At some point

I just stopped taking them off. Hey, I don't mind being up high anymore. If I fall I can grab a hunk of cloud and parachute down.

Of course, I'm speaking metaphorically…or allegorically. I sit down hard. How am I speaking…elliptically? Transcendentally? My brain is leaking. There goes all that word power, down the tube.

Oh well—no big deal. I am suddenly aware of a more urgent matter. I have to pee.

I almost piss off the edge of the roof. Honest to God. Another beer and I'd do it. And there's something else… Oh, yeah, got to catch a bus.

I swing my arm up and check the time. Big hand is on the nine, little hand on the four—four and a half. "Lonny? Would you come over here a second?"

I hear him lay the hammer down. As he steps over the roof peak to my side he nods his approval. "Great work, man, you really got it going."

"Speaking of going…" I tap the glass on my watch. "It's about that time"

He shifts his weight. "Is there a later bus?"

I pull the crumpled schedule out of my jeans, close one eye, and read it. "There's a ten-forty."

"How about you catch that one? It'd be a shame to knock off now."

"I don't know…." My inner straight-A student is having a panic attack. "That'll get me in super late, and the bus station was already Twilight Zone at eight in the morning."

"Shee-it!" He slaps my back. "You aren't afraid of a few winos. We've still got daylight. Let's run it out."

Catching the later bus, I'd get maybe three hours of sleep—but I've done school on less than that plenty of times. Still, it would be better to go now.

I'm about to make that clear when Lonny looks at me out of the corner of his eye. "I know Sissy would appreciate it."

Her hammer is tap-tapping on the other side of the roof; what's a few more hours? "You'll drive me to the ten-forty?"

"You know I will."

"Okay. Why the hell not?" We bump fists in a show of roofers' solidarity. The inner straight-A guy lets out a little girly scream.

When Lonny gets to his own side of the roof he yells "Heads up!" and tosses another can of beer over the roof peak at me. I execute a smooth catch.

I don't lose much when it geysers out of the can—what misses my mouth drenches my chest. Strangely refreshing. But there's some urgent business to attend to. I listen to make sure that Sissy is still hammering, then walk to the roof edge and water something so far below I can't even see it.

Lonny and I stand with the roof peak under our arches. "Not a bad day's work," he says, hanging an arm around my shoulders.

The sun is a glow behind the big oak. The courses of shingles Sissy and I nailed don't cover much. Still, in the raking light, they look neat and even. We turn toward the second side, half of which I've taken down to the sheathing. "If it rains now it'll leak big-time," I observe.

"Like a son of a bitch," he agrees. "But I don't see any clouds, do you?" He pulls his T-shirt back on and tosses empty cans into the yard. "Quit borrowing trouble."

"I wish I could stick around, see the job through."

"Then do it."

"I can't," I say quickly. "But I've never done this kind of work before—work you can see. Maybe after college I'll join the Peace Corps, build a few things."

"Peace Corps, huh? Is that where smart guys go to do roofs?"

6

onny and Sissy are both buzzed—guess I am too. There's a lot of giggling at supper. All Charlie knows is that his parents are happy, so he's happy. He laughs so hard a hunk of bread goes down the wrong tube. I have to Heimlich him—even that seems funny.

They're still laughing as I carry the phone to the top of the stairs and sit down, grinning; one last call to Dad before I head home.

Dad picks up on the first ring, "Fisher! Where've you been? I've been trying to reach you for a couple of hours. I was about to call Mrs. Zelinsky and have her check on you."

Why doesn't he trust me? "I was studying with Hofstra. What did you think?" At least statistically it's true. I study so much that there must be some parallel Fisher who's doing it right now.

"All kinds of things happen to kids these days—"

"Dad, I'm sixteen, I can handle all kinds of things." All I did was steal a couple of days from my own life. I'm entitled.

We talk pointlessly for a while longer. I cut it short when the family moves to the living room. The voices are louder now. The TV comes on. "Call you tomorrow, Dad."

"Oh, okay. Just one more thing. How is Desiree?"

"Fine."

We hang up. I sit on the step, tossing the phone from hand to hand. I've hardly thought about Dez and her dead dog since I left Tallahassee. I'll make up for it tomorrow when we share our seat on Number 47 and my life drops back into its usual groove.

"Hey, Fish!" I hear Charlie run across the living room.

"Hey what?" I shout back.

He pounds up the stairs and falls into me. I wrap my arms around him and hug him hard.

"Fi-ish!" he objects when I start to tickle.

"Wha-at?" I tickle harder. Lonny should be doing this. He's the dad. This is what dads do. But then I try to remember horsing around with my own father, and I can't. Life with Dad is one long conversation-with-a-purpose. Mom was more fun. I hold onto Charlie's squirming arms and growl, "Give up or die, you evil weenie!"

"Okay, okay!" We're both panting, both grinning when we quit struggling. "Can you read me another book with your eyes closed, Fish?"

"Maybe. Is it bedtime?"

"I dunno."

"Let's check." As I stand, I heft him up onto my shoulders. I can tell he's scared and thrilled at the same time. He whoops and grabs my hair. When I hold his skinny legs to steady him they feel electric.

"Hey!" he shouts again. "You know what? I can touch the ceiling!"

"That's because you plus me equals one giant!" And we thump down the stairs.

"Here comes the giant!" Charlie yells. "The great big *scary* giant!"

The big scary giant strides into the living room—and stops. My face gets hot when I realize what's happening on the couch—not that I get much of a look before Charlie slaps his hands over my glasses.

"Charlie, let Fish see!" Sissy orders.

When Charlie puts his hands down, his parents aren't making out anymore, but Sissy's shirt is untucked on one side. "We're just watching TV," she says, retucking it.

It doesn't look like Lonny will be sleeping on the couch tonight. "Guess you knew what you were doing when you bought that one-way ticket," I tell him quietly.

I am such an idiot. I'm not part of this family. Except to Charlie, I'm just two days of free labor. My real life is the one where I'm studying with Hofstra. "Don't get too comfortable," I warn Lonny.

"Got ya covered," he says.

"Good." Then, because I don't know what else to do, I offer to put Charlie to bed. Sissy thanks me, then makes Lonny say good night to Charlie—that doesn't take long. And the scary giant stumbles back up the stairs. On the sofa,

I assume they pick up where they left off. It gets awfully quiet.

I help Charlie into his pajamas. It's time for me to tell him that I'm leaving—this night's shaping up just great. But I don't want him to wake up tomorrow and think I baled on him. I put it off when he demands that I read him another story with my eyes closed. I do *Horton Hatches the Egg.* I'm not as good at Horton as I am at *The Cat in the Hat*—which is how I discover that Charlie can read. I open my eyes and he points out the spot where I got the words wrong, then reads the rest of the book to me. "When did you learn to read?"

He shrugs. "I kind of always knew how."

"It was like that for me too." For a second I want to take him with me. Dad would get used to it—he likes smart kids—but Sissy wouldn't. He can't come with me but I've got to go. I'm about to tell him when he closes the book. "Want to see something?" he whispers.

"What kind of something?"

He reaches under his pillow. "This." He holds out a fossil as big as my palm.

"Awesome!"

"It's a sloth toenail." He puts it in my hand and leans against me and we both examine it.

"I have a collection at home in my closet. It's mostly sharks' teeth. They're pretty easy to find. I have one that's super huge."

"Wow!" he breathes as I spread my fingers a good inch and a half wider than the actual specimen.

"It's not as cool as this," I admit. I turn the sloth toenail over in my hand, balancing it on my palm. "I always wanted one of these."

He tries to fold my fingers over it. "You take it for a while. We can share."

"Thanks, but you better keep it. I have to go home pretty soon."

He stiffens. "When soon?"

"Tonight." He doesn't answer, but that doesn't mean that it doesn't matter. "Looks like your dad and mom are working things out," I offer.

There's a long pause before he answers, "We'll see." He sounds like a cautious old man, not a kid. But he's probably right. Kids know these things. I give him one last hug and reach up and turn out the light.

A shout erupts from downstairs. "You are so full of it, Lonny Traynor!"

"See?" says Charlie. In the weak glow of the nightlight I can see the startled whites of his eyes.

The voices drop, but only for a few seconds. "Don't give me that! You never paid attention to Charlie, never, ever."

"I'm not into kids!" Lonny's raised voice sounds surprised and hurt. "You knew that. I told you from the get-go—you have 'em, they're yours."

Charlie curls up against my chest. "It's the beer," I say. "He doesn't mean it."

"Yes, he does. He doesn't like me."

An adult would say, *yes he does,* but I'm not going to bullshit him. "Your mom loves you, though, big-time. Mine got tired of me and went away."

He lifts his head off my chest. "Do you have a dad?"

"Yeah. That's who I live with."

"Maybe your dad and my mom could get together."

It's the simple kind of plan a kid comes up with. Right after my mother left, Desiree and I had the same idea: her mom, my dad, Boots and Walt, like there was ever a chance. "I don't think it would work," I tell him gently. "My dad's too old for your mom."

"Maybe not too, too, too old."

"He's sort of bald."

"Oh."

"I know it's a serious responsibility!" Lonny yells. "I'm doing the roof, aren't I?"

I give Charlie a nudge. "Let's get out of here."

I toss his blanket out the window ahead of us and climb out. When I turn around his pale face seems to float in the dark window. "Mom doesn't let me go on the roof."

"It's okay. You'll be with me." I take his hands and help him out. Then I close the window and lift him into my lap. We can still hear the shouting but we can't make out the words.

"It's hard being a kid," I tell Charlie, who is staring at the moon. "But you won't always be one. Someday *you'll* be in charge." I don't even know if he's listening. Still staring at the moon, he pulls his fist back to his shoulder and does the swimming sperm thing. "What does that mean, Charlie?"

"It's the dying comet."

"How come you and your dad have a signal for a dying comet?"

He shrugs against me. "We just do. We made it up together. Some days he likes me, Fish."

"You bet he does."

Just not enough. I pull the blanket around both of us and hold him. Even in my scrawny arms, he sure feels small.

I wake up with a start. My neck is stiff, one leg is numb. Charlie's asleep against my chest. I listen, but the fight downstairs seems to be over. All of a sudden, a fist of adrenaline pounds the middle of my chest. How late is it? I rock Charlie's head off my arm and check the lit dial on my watch.

Crap! In fourteen and one-half minutes I need to be at Bett's. I turn toward the window. Maybe I can put Charlie in bed without waking him up. I'm about to try when inside his room I see movement. A shadowy shape leans over his pillow.

I knock on the glass and hear a stifled scream.

The window flies up. "What in the world are you two doing out here?" Sissy demands.

"Getting away from the fight."

For a moment she just stands with her arms raised, hands on the window sash. "We were yelling, weren't we? *I* was yelling. I can't let him do that to me," she says softly. She puts a knee on the sill and crawls out onto the roof. "But he makes me *so* mad."

We could sit out here a long time. I may be gut clueless like Dez says, but even I can tell she needs to talk. Hell, *I* need to talk. But I can't miss my bus. "Sissy, you have to drive me to Bett's right now. I have to catch the bus. I have school tomorrow."

"I thought you were on break or something. Didn't Larry send you to help?"

"No, I'm not really Cousin Larry's kid."

She stares. "Now what good did it do him to lie about that? I swear, lying's a hobby with that man. If you're not Lonny's cousin, who are you?"

"Lonny's brother Dave is my neighbor."

"Dave asked you to help?"

"No, Lonny invited me along for a weekend adventure. He knew I needed a break."

"A weekend adventure?" She covers her face and laughs. As her shoulders shake it's hard to tell whether she's laughing or crying. "He had a roof to put on and he needed help. He conned you, Fish."

"No, really, I don't think so. At least not completely."

"Yes, completely. He promised you an adventure, but what's your big adventure been so far? You got to sweat on a roof for a couple of beers. Whoopee."

"You're not taking into account meeting you and Charlie…."

"Oh, yeah," she says. "That's a real life-changer. Trust me, Fish, Lonny looks out for Lonny."

"Maybe so," I admit. "Still, I had a good time. I wish I could stay—but I can't. I really have to go—like right now." I hold out my wrist to show her the glowing dial.

Instead of reading the watch she grasps my hand in both of hers. "No, Fish, don't go, please. Mad as he is, if you bail, he'll cut and run and if it rains the water will just pour right through this roof."

In the moonlight I can see that the shingles we nailed today cover basically nothing, just the eaves and a little way in from the front wall. The house would flood in a downpour, but I can't help her. "You don't understand about me and school.... I can't screw up. I need a scholarship—"

"One day," she begs, "just give me one day, Fish! Don't you ever get sick?"

"Sure, but I go anyway." Dad and I call it playing hurt. "I haven't missed a day of high school yet."

"Then one day shouldn't be a problem. Please. Stick around for one more day so I can smooth things over with Lonny and get him to finish the job. Everyone misses school once in a while."

I turn toward her to talk her out of believing that I can stay. But she's quit trying to convince me. Arms wrapped around her knees, she stares at the moon. "I can't do this anymore," she breathes. "I can't keep it going all by myself. Where do I go to give up?"

"Wish I knew," I whisper back. I think about it myself sometimes.

The seconds are falling away. I've got to go now, before now, hours ago. I should never have come in the first place. But I'm here and she needs help.

I run a quick hypothetical. Let's just say I miss tomorrow. Worst-case scenario, something might be covered I'll need for an exam. Unless Hofstra has totally melted down, he's taking notes in the critical classes. Minor complication: He takes notes in mirror writing—everything backwards, like Leonardo da Vinci. But I have a mirror.

Other possible repercussions? Living with Dad I know them all. Students at Leon are allowed three unexcused absences in a class, no questions asked, so I could miss one day—one unexcused absence per class, and I don't even have all of my classes on Monday. But still—my perfect record shimmers like a brand new car sitting on the lot.

I feel Charlie's deep, long breaths against my chest, I see the gleam of tears in Sissy's eyes as she stares at the moon—and I drive that car right off the lot and into the first telephone pole I see. "One day. I can give you one more day, but that's all."

"Really, you'd do that for me?" She sounds as if she's afraid to hope.

"Who needs a perfect attendance record, anyway? But you have to put me on the five o'clock tomorrow night. Not Lonny, you."

"Girl Scout's honor." She gives me the three-finger scout salute, then pulls her hands inside the sleeves of her sweater.

"Come on." I hold out one side of the blanket. She scoots over. With my arm around her shoulders we're all wrapped up together: Charlie, Sissy, and me.

7

aucity: scarcity...dearth...insufficiency." I glance up from *Word Power* and catch sight of the bread bag on the counter. The plastic is knotted above four slices of bread. There's a paucity, scarcity, dearth, *and* insufficiency of food in this house. If it weren't for leftovers from the diner there'd be almost nothing to eat—but I can't fix that. I can only give Sissy a day. After that I have to go.

I'd like to stride into the living room, dump Lonny's lazy ass off the couch, and get started, but it isn't even light yet.

I slide my finger down to the next word on the page. "Platonic: of or relating to a relationship between a man and a woman that is purely spiritual or intellectual and without sexual activity."

Which would describe my relationship with every woman on the planet. I teach them math, I carry their dead dogs, I fix their roofs. Just call me Fisher Platonic Brown.

Although she pads into the kitchen quietly, Sissy doesn't take me by surprise this time. I guess I've been waiting for her. Her right cheek is pink. Must be the one that rested on the pillow. Eyes half closed, she gives me a weak wave, then gropes for the glass pot on the coffeemaker. She stands at the sink and fills it with a thin stream from the tap. I'm about to tell her it would go faster if she opened up the faucet, but I notice that her head is resting against the cabinet over the sink, her eyes are closed. When the water runs over she whispers, "Shit," and opens them.

While the coffee drips she sits opposite me at the table. She rests her weight on her crossed arms and leans toward me. "Thanks for still being here," she says softly.

"You thought I'd sneak out in the night? That's the other guy."

She picks up the index card I've been using as a bookmark; I tore it off the wall and stuck it in when I decided to hit the road. "The longest journey begins with a single step," she reads.

"Advice from my dad. He tapes these tips all over my room, his way of operating me by remote control."

"I think it's nice. Like having a guardian angel."

I wish she could see into my life the way I see into hers. "Guardian angels—assuming they exist—hover around hoping for the best. They don't exert pressure."

She turns the card toward me. "This is pressure?"

"One of the more benign manifestations."

"Wish I had someone watching over me." She reads the card again. "The longest journey begins with a single step." She sighs and drops the card on the table. "For me the first step leads to Bett's and the next step leads home."

"It's like that for me too: home to school, school to home, home to—"

She puts her hand on mine and gives it a quick squeeze. "But that's just for now. Next comes college, a good job. You're going somewhere, Fish. All I'm doing is wearing the pattern off the linoleum at Bett's." She rests her head on her arms.

Her hopelessness seeps into me. One day isn't going to roof her house. Two or three wouldn't do it either. And fixing the roof won't fix what's wrong. Her situation is a black hole. I'm afraid I'll get sucked in—and I'm just as scared that when I leave I'll never see her or Charlie again.

Borrowing one from Lonny I think, Let tonight take care of tonight. "You look like you need a cup of coffee." She doesn't lift her head off her arms until I nudge the back of her hand with a warm mug. "Come on. Elixir of Life!"

"Thanks," she mouths. She takes a sip, then stands, pushing the chair back quietly. It's clear that today she doesn't want to wake the sleeping water buffalo on the couch, afraid they'll get into it again and Lonny will leave. Together we put out milk, cereal, bowls. We do everything as if we were moving underwater, slowly and in near-silence, a silence Charlie blows when he wanders down to the kitchen and discovers that I'm still here. "I thought you just forgot your pants on the bed!" He throws himself at my legs and hangs on.

"Nope, me and the pants stick together." I should tell him that me and the pants will be out of here this evening, but he's happy. Let tonight take care of tonight.

"I have to make a phone call," I say, peeling him off. "Got to tell my friend Desiree I won't be in school today."

"Your girlfriend?" asks Sissy with a sly smile.

I hold up both hands. "Friend, just a friend. It's strictly platonic."

Seated on the top step of the staircase I dial and listen to the buzz of the phone ringing on the coffee table in front of the TV at Dez's. I hope I get her sister or Boots. It'll be easier to lie.

"Hello?"

Bummer, it's Dez. "Hey."

"Fisher! Thanks a lot for returning my calls. I left you, like, forty messages."

"Yeah, well…" Some woman newscaster is talking in the background. Probably *Good Morning America*. The TV is always on at the Swanson's.

"Yeah, well, what?" she asks.

For a second I think of claiming I'm sick—which would be wise if anyone tells Dad I missed a day, but she knows about my perfect record. She'll assume I'm dying. After school she'll rush over to take my temperature, force fluids or whatever, and I won't be there. "I'm not at home, Dez. I'm…I'm in Miami with Dad."

"Get out! You went with him?" A voice that isn't reporting the national news whines about earrings. "No," says Dez, sounding exasperated. "I don't know where your earrings are. Check the back of the toilet… So, you went with him? Why the change of plan?"

"It was kind of last second. We're packing up the house now." I can't believe it. I'm getting good at lying, almost as smooth as Lonny.

But why push it. "How are *you* doing?" I ask, changing the subject fast. "I mean…are you getting along okay without the Beaner?"

Even over the blab of the TV, I hear her inhale sharply. She finally answers, "I'm alive."

"I wish I could be there to cheer you up."

"Yeah, yeah. Just get your butt back here." She snuffs and I wonder if she's crying. If she is, it doesn't keep her from yelling, "They're not on the back of the toilet? Maybe they fell in! Fisher, I better go. Precious is having a fashion melt-down. Give your dad a hug."

But I don't want her to hang up. "That was rhetorical, right? The Brown family is a no-hug zone—an ordinance you seriously broke, by the way."

"Fisher, you are abundantly full of crap." Only Dez can make "full of crap" sound like a term of endearment.

I listen to her breathe for a couple of seconds, then add, "Miss you. Bye." I hang up before she can say anything else. She's right. I am abundantly full of crap. I left the "I" off because "I miss you" sounds like a commitment—but hearing her voice, I do miss her. What am I doing here?

131

I creep back down the stairs and return the phone to its cradle as quietly as possible, but Lonny's snoring keeps any sound I make from waking him up. When I get to the kitchen it's empty. Through the window I see Sissy dragging a hose across the yard. Charlie's already in the backseat of the car. She's taking off without even a thanks-for-torpedoing-your-perfect-record-on-my-behalf? Or at least a goodbye? I feel cheated.

I close the front door gently and walk up behind her. "Sissy?"

"Talk fast, Fish. Sorry, but I'm running late." She smacks the hood of the car with both palms. Nothing happens. "I can see what kind of a day *this* is going to be," she mutters. "Beat on the other side, okay?" We wham the hood until something inside springs loose and the hood pops up. She raises it and uncaps the radiator, then shoves the nozzle into the fill and pulls the trigger. "I get off at two," she shouts over the spraying water. "Keep Lonny here until I get back. Nail him to the roof if you have to."

"And the five o'clock bus?"

She doesn't answer, just holds up those three Girl Scout fingers.

The rear window on the car squeaks down. "Fish? Can we do Erectors when I get home?"

"You'll see Fish after school," says Sissy, a safe, diplomatic answer that covers a lie. Seeing me after school won't include Erectors. It'll be about saying goodbye.

"See you when you get home," I tell him, crossing over to the dark side too. But he's smiling when he rolls the window back up. Let tonight take care of tonight.

Sissy tosses the hose down, caps the radiator, and slams the hood. She rushes to the driver's door, opens it, then stops. "Missing school is a big thing for you, isn't it?"

"Not as big as donating a kidney." I'm still standing in front of the car.

She walks slowly over to me and puts her arms around my neck and whispers, "Thank you, thank you."

"You're welcome, welcome." I wrap my arms around her waist and hold her against me. I hold her longer than I should, and too tight. I mumble, "Sorry," and let go.

She steps away from me, not meeting my eyes. For a second she fusses with her uniform, smoothing it, then she grabs my wrist with two fingers and checks my watch. "Shoot! Gotta go!" She goes up on her toes. Her lips graze my cheek. "Bye!"

I walk back to the house in a daze. Suddenly I feel that, with total focus, Lonny and I can get the roof done, at least the one side. If we work straight through and forget breaks, it could happen. The screen door hasn't even slapped shut when I yell, "Rise and shine, Lonny. We're burning daylight." I hear a groan from the living room, then the sound of a naked man hopping on one foot, wrestling with his jeans.

He stumbles into the kitchen and helps himself to the last of the coffee. Then he drains the sugar bowl into the mug. "I hope you have a damned good reason for getting me up before the birds."

"The birds have been up for hours. Just chug it, okay? Let's get started."

"Slow down there, quick-draw. Let me inhale some of this first." He thumps his chest with a fist. "Gotta get the old heart pumping. Thought you had to be in school today."

"I do, but I—Sissy begged me to help her out."

"Oh…" Lonny nods knowingly. "I can just imagine that scene. She can be very persuasive when she sets her mind to it."

"I was stranded here anyway, thanks to you. Come on, we have work to do."

But if he's feeling remorse it doesn't show. He falls into a kitchen chair and props his feet on the table. "You know how to strip shingles. I'll be up in a few."

When I get to the roof and stand facing into the cool damp breeze, I make an executive decision. Instead of stripping shingles, which would be taking things in the wrong direction, I try to replicate Sissy's neat rows of shingles with strips of my own, laying them out evenly but fast. I've finished a whole row before I realize I'm still wearing my glasses and I'm not even drunk. I guess I've totally adjusted to the altitude. A small gain, but it's something.

I check my watch. At home I'd be in English now, contemplating Chaucer. Here, I'm contemplating the vastness of the roof and wondering where the hell Lonny is. I stick my head in the window and bawl, "Lonny, get your ass up here!"

It's a good twenty minutes before I hear him clump through Charlie's room. The first thing to come out the window is his fist, holding a couple of beers. "Here you go. Breakfast of champions." He rolls one down the roof to me.

I set it upright but don't pull the tab. He doesn't comment. "Keep nailing, Fish. I'll strip."

"How about if we both nail, get one side done in case it rains?"

He scans the sky. "Nah. Let's keep pushing." He carries a shovel to the other side of the roof.

I nail until the heel of the hand that rests on the hammer gets numb—then nail some more.

"How'd she get you to stay?" he asks when we eat lunch. "A big wet kiss on the lips?"

I just stare at him until his grin fades. "Let's get back to work."

He slaps his knees and stands up. "Well, if it isn't Saint Fish." We walk back to our jobs on opposite sides of the roof.

Neat and even, the rows of shingles slowly add up, but by two o'clock I'm only a third of the way up the roof. Meanwhile, on the other side, Lonny is opening up more of Sissy's house to the sky. A few clouds have formed since we've been up here. So far they're innocuous, fluffy, and white. They look like the cumulus cloud diagram from some elementary school meteorology unit. But cumulus can go bad, turn cumulonimbus, unleashing thunder, lightning, rain.

"I have to head home tonight!" I shout. "You'd better stick around and finish the job." All that rises above the roof peak is a tattooed arm, middle finger pointed toward the sky.

"If you don't," I add, "I'll come back and help Rhoda hunt you down and kill you."

"I'm shakin', Fish."

Ten minutes later he tosses down his shovel. "Let me see if I can scare us up a couple more beers." And he climbs back through Charlie's window.

Every few minutes I check my watch, but lifting my arm is getting to be work. I set the hammer down and my right arm hangs at my side like it's filled with sand. My fingers are swollen. I seriously doubt whether I could even hold a pencil. But I pick the hammer up and keep going.

When he's been gone an hour I think, why wait for Rhoda? I go inside to hunt him down and kill him. "Lonny?" I expect to find him crashed somewhere, but the house is eerily quiet.

I push the front door open. "Lonny?" The cordless phone sits in the cane seat of the rocker on the porch. He must've called someone, maybe even tried to get a ride. But I would have heard a car pull up. I would have seen it.

I take the phone inside and set it in its cradle. Expecting the worst, I check behind the sofa, but his duffle still leans against the wall. I go back to nailing shingles, inching my way up the roof. I don't know what else to do.

I'm still nailing when Sissy and Charlie pull into the yard.

I wave at her as she climbs out of the car, but she's not looking at me; she's looking at the guy who isn't there. Over her head the growing herd of clouds is not so benign any more. They're flat on the bottom and dark, shifting toward the next diagram in the book, the thuggish cumulonimbus.

My response is what it's been all day: I pick up another strip of shingles. I'm positioning the first nail when I hear her scurry up the steps. "Where is he, Fish?"

"He went inside to get beer a couple hours ago. I haven't seen him since."

She practically leaps through the window, her eyes wild. "Why didn't you stop him?"

"Why are you yelling at *me?*" I yell back. "I'm the guy who's still here!"

Charlie's small, unhappy face appears at the window. "Don't fight!"

Sissy doesn't look at him but she lowers her voice. "You *knew* he was going to split."

"He said he was looking for beer. I'm not a mind reader."

She looks at the rows of shingles I've been nailing non-stop since she left, and bites her lip.

"What do you want? My hand's numb!" To help her, I'm missing my first day of school since seventh grade. But does she appreciate it? "I'm nailing as fast as I can."

"Did he do anything at all?"

"He was working on the other side."

She lets out a gasp and clambers to the other side of the roof. I follow her slowly, knowing what she'll see when she gets there.

Her back is to me, her fists clenched at her sides. All of the old shingles have been torn off. I step past her down the roof and face her. I'm taller than any girl I've ever met—the girl's-eye view of Fisher Brown is usually straight up the nose—but because I'm standing further down the slope, Sissy is gazing directly into my eyes. If this were a movie the irresistible force of magnetic lip attraction would make a kiss virtually inevitable.

Shit. Lonny is getting into my head. Lonny and his big wet kiss on the lips.

"Is he trying to sabotage us?" she moans. A breeze pours over the roof, blowing a loose strand of hair across her face. I want to sweep it aside with my fingers, but squeeze my hands in my back pockets instead. What she sees in front of her is a skinny high school kid with thick glasses and weird hair—a platonic roof guy.

"It's going to rain, isn't it?" she whispers. As if saying the word makes it real, all of a sudden I smell rain on the wind.

"Just a quick shower, maybe…" But the black sky says I'm lying. "I only have an hour before I have to catch the bus…. You know I can't stay."

"I know, I know. But, before you go, help me cover the roof."

"With what?"

She points to the pile of blue plastic bunched next to the roofing supplies on the ground. I go down and drag it back up the stairs.

"It's too small to cover much," I say as the blue tarp billows between us. It's like spreading a tablecloth.

"Just cover Charlie."

"Won't the water run under it?" I ask, but she's already tacking it over the section of roof that shelters Charlie's bed.

Knowing it won't do a bit of good, I help her.

"What are you going to do?" I ask as she drives me into town.

"Don't know."

But she must have some kind of plan. She grabbed the tip jar as we left the house.

"You going to pick up a bigger tarp?"

"And who would help me nail it down?"

"Me, Mommy," Charlie pipes from the backseat.

"How about Rhoda?" I ask.

"Rhoda has three little kids, nobody to watch them."

Rain spatters the windshield. "A neighbor, anybody?"

Hands locked tight to the steering wheel, her back a foot from the seat, she stares at the road and thinks. "There's Roland next door, but I wouldn't want to give him any encouragement. Forget it, Fish. It's not your problem."

It isn't my problem—but it is. Like Dad burying Desiree's dog, things become your problem when there's no one else. "Put me on the ten-forty, Sissy, I'll help."

She turns, startled. "Really?"

"Yes, really." The smile she flashes me makes facing the winos in the middle of the night and falling asleep at my desk in school tomorrow seem like a good deal. "Now, fly like the wind! To Wal-Mart!"

She whoops, "Yee-haw!" and jams the gas pedal.

We need not one, but two big tarps. Forty-eight dollars plus tax. She pays the last seventeen dollars with change, a glacially slow process that doesn't thrill the line waiting behind us. The quarters don't take long, but she quickly gets down to the dimes and nickels and pennies. I watch the gray slab of sky out the front window of the store while Charlie arranges the messy heaps of change into neat stacks for the cashier. I'd like to whip out my money and pay but decide I'd better hang onto it—I'm not home yet.

Back in the parking lot the car won't start. Sissy twists the key over and over, like the next time the action will elicit something more useful than a faint click.

She falls back against the seat staring up at the sagging headliner. "What did I ever do to you, God?"

"I can fix it." I sound more confident than I feel. Luckily, this time the hood pops without her help. The battery terminals are crusted with white. This battery is old, leaky, and on its way out. I do the only trick I know; I jiggle the leads back and forth, shout, "Heal!" and hold up a hand. "That should do it. Try again." Miracle of miracles, it starts.

"Works every time," I say, and we cruise home with the wipers on intermittent.

Sissy holds the waist of my jeans; we lean into the wind. The knot of roofing nails in my pocket bites into my thigh. Pins of rain sting my neck. Like a nightmare, the roof seems to be getting steeper. I left my glasses in Charlie's room, not to trick myself—seeing would actually be desirable under these circumstances—but because in the rain they'll make me even more blind.

"What should we do?" she shouts.

I wonder why she asks. How hard can it be to spread a tarp? I hand her a corner and take one myself. "Walk yours that way," I shout back.

We've barely stepped away from each other when the wind inflates the tarp with a snap. I hear Sissy's scream over the rip and flap of plastic. Pulled by the force of the wind, she's sliding down the roof. "Get down, Sissy. Drop!"

She falls on her side and I lunge across the plastic, trying to mash it flat against the roof to keep it from taking off. Lonny's warning about walking on loose shingles comes back—like stepping on a banana peel, he said. A wet tarp is worse. I slide head-first as the plastic slips against the bare plywood. The toes of my sneakers drag against the roof; I try like mad to brake. My feet, not on the plastic, are slowing me down, but I'm still heading for the edge. The brain is telling me to roll off the tarp, to let it blow away, but the body is in a full panic lockdown, so I keep digging my toes in, keep inching down, as the rain soaks my back.

I cut the distance to the edge of the roof in half, then in half again. Keep cutting a distance in half and, at least in theory, you never get there. Zeno's paradox. But life and theory are parting ways. The sheet of plastic lashes in the open air and the roof beneath my left hand disappears.

Dad and Dez flash across my brain—my pitiful 4.80 GPA

life, over before it started—then I remember I'm not alone up here. "Sissy!" I shout.

Oh god, don't let me take her with me.

Something clamps my ankle and the slide stops. Time stops. The plastic bunches under me as I'm dragged back from the edge. One moment ago death felt like a pane of glass my face was pressed against. Now it recedes.

I roll off the tarp. With a massive flap the plastic sheet takes off, like a flight of pterodactyls.

"Hey, Snowflake, you okay?" I can just make out Lonny, squatting on the roof. Rain drips off his chin. He leans across and with his free hand grasps my wrist and pulls me to a sitting position.

"Oh god! Where's Sissy?" We're the only ones on the roof.

"I sent her inside. I couldn't believe my eyes when I got back from Roland's and saw the two of you sliding around up here like the Ice Capades."

"Roland's?" I shout. "What the hell were you doing there?"

"We were out of beer. I went to bum a couple. We got talking."

"Talking?"

Hand on the back of my neck, he jerks my face right up to his to be sure I can hear him over the pounding rain. "Get righteous on me later, okay? We've got a roof to cover."

You bet I'll get righteous. As soon as I can see and I'm not breathing rain, I'll show him righteous.

With Lonny in charge, we stay low and keep the plastic

pressed to the roof. We unfold the second tarp and nail it in place as we go. When we get to the other side, I shout, "We need the tarp that took off. I'll go get it." But Sissy must have seen it take off and chased it down. She stuffs the tarp through the window. This one's harder to spread since it's wet and wadded up, but Lonny makes sure we keep it down so the wind never gets ahold of it.

Sitting at my desk at home, I would have come up with the same solution. I'm great, as long as the problem's on paper. But how often is any real problem on paper?

"Roland's?" Sissy shoves a mug of hot coffee at Lonny. "Why the hell were you at Roland's?"

"Beer!" I say. "He went to get beer!"

Lonny cocks a boot heel on the edge of the kitchen table. His dripping pant leg is shaggy with burrs. "Why the hell not?"

She slaps the boot off the table. "Because you were supposed to be working on the roof. Fish is missing school!"

"Missing a day or two won't hurt him."

"That's one day." I squeeze the bottom of my T-shirt over the sink. "*One*. The job is all yours now. And you damned well better stick around and do it." I sit down across from him.

Under the table the pointy toe of a boot pokes me in the thigh. "Thought I split, didn't you?"

Behind me Sissy slams a cupboard door. "Wouldn't be the first time."

Lonny turns on her so fast he almost upsets the chair. "How did I ever get tangled up with you, girl? You're so damned suspicious, I—"

"Hold it!" I say. "Just hold it." I point toward the living room where Charlie is watching a video and we all hear the tinny *Sesame Street* jingle: *Sunny day, chasing the clouds away...* "You two have to cut this out."

Sissy slams another cupboard door.

"I mean it, both of you! Control yourselves! You have a kid in there."

"Look out," Lonny says with a laugh. "This boy's up on his hind legs now!"

"This is *not* a joke." I try my best to sound like Dad—like their behavior has consequences. "He's your son!" I pause and look at each of them. "When you fight like this you hurt him." I take my phone card out of a damp pocket. "If you'll excuse me, I have to lie to my dad now. Don't let me hear you two yell at each other."

While I tell Dad I had spaghetti for supper, I keep one ear tuned in to the kitchen. But at least for now, all is quiet.

Ten o'clock. My pack hangs heavy from my shoulders—half the clothes inside are soaked and wrapped in trash bags. I said goodbye to Charlie when I put him to bed. I read him *The Lorax.* He'll miss our nightly Seussfest; do anything more than once with a kid and it becomes tradition. He hugged me around the neck so hard he almost severed my air supply. I didn't mind.

I lift the pack straps and resettle them. "See you in Talla-hassee?" I ask Lonny.

"Ya never know." He holds out an arm.

"You going to finish the roof?"

"You want it written in blood?"

"Blood would be good." I grab his arm with a slap, lock-ing into the same secret biker handshake we started out with. I give the blue snake a hard squeeze, then let go, pretty sure I'll never see him again.

Sissy jangles the keys. "It's still raining hard. We better take off."

"I'll drive him," Lonny offers, following us as far as the porch.

"Not a chance," says Sissy.

Standing on the porch, I turn and take one last look at the house. Someone should replace the torn screen in the door. Someone should change the burnt-out bulb.

"You know, you could stay," says Lonny, reading my head.

"Afraid not."

He slouches against a porch column. "Then this is where you make your big exit."

"This would be it." It all seems so anti-climactic that I jump off the porch with a yelp and run through the rain. I fall, dripping, into the car. In a second the driver's side door whips open and Sissy drops into the driver seat. "Where to?" she asks.

I put a sneaker up on the dashboard. "Surprise me." But we both know the game is over. She'll drive me to Bett's. I'll doze my way back to Tallahassee, trip over the winos in the bus station, and be talking to Lynelle's face in the rearview mirror and checking out the drawing on Desiree's arm first thing tomorrow.

It's time to loop.

Then Sissy tries to start the car. When nothing happens she digs a flashlight out of the glove compartment. "Do what you did before," she says. I jiggle the battery wires until my back is soaked. After watching me fail for a decent length of time Lonny comes down the steps. He tries too, but no amount of magic fingers on the terminal wires can convince the engine to turn over.

"No!" says Sissy, opening the driver's door and scrambling out. "This is not going to happen. I promised you you'd get home, Fish!"

"What's another day?" Lonny calls after her as she rushes back to the house. "He's cool with it. You're cool with it, right?"

My head still under the hood, I breathe the tired-grease smell of the engine. "I am in such deep-shit trouble." When I look toward the house Sissy is on the porch, the phone pressed to her ear. She paces. Whoever she's calling isn't picking up. She throws the handset into the rocker, runs back down the steps, and grabs the flashlight out of my hand. "Be right back!" She dashes for the line of trees beyond the house.

"Look at that girl go!" marvels Lonny. "She's gonna hustle you up a ride with Roland—and she doesn't even like the man." He claps a hand on my shoulder. "No sense getting soaked while we wait." We sprint back to the house. He goes inside but I stay on the porch, like that will make things happen faster.

It isn't long before the scrub oaks at the edge of the woods shake and the flashlight beam reappears. It bobs across the dark yard. "He wasn't there!" Sissy takes the steps two at a time and throws the flashlight into the rocker. Gulping as she tries to catch her breath, she grabs both my hands. "I am so sorry!" Her wet hair is matted to her head. I notice the way her ears stick out a little, her eyelashes clump. "I don't know what to do!" she moans.

Lonny cocks the door open with his shoulder. "Come on inside, you two. Fish'll get there tomorrow, what's the difference?"

Sleep is not going to happen. I lie on the bed across the room from Charlie's and think. Two unexcused absences. Two I can get away with. No one questions two. I'm still okay. Nothing catastrophic has happened yet. I'm the same student I was on Friday; nothing's changed.

I'm shaking—I can feel the metal frame of the bed rattle against the wall—but it's because I'm cold. I've never been this cold or tired in my life. I close my eyes, knowing it won't do any good.

I wake up once in the night. Charlie's crawled into bed with me. I try to remember being in my own bed at home, but all that is real right now is the slightly musty smell of the top of Charlie's head and his lispy breathing. My life back home is like a line someone is erasing behind me.

Listening to Charlie breathe, I think, was it like this for Mom? Maybe she planned to come back but one thing happened and then another, and maybe when she turned around, the line that was her life with me and Dad was gone.

It won't be like that for me. If I keep it down to two unexcused absences I'm still solid. Solid like it never happened.

8

"Hey." Lonny jostles my shoulder. "Get dressed. I'm gonna scare us up a ride."

I open my eyes. I'm still curled around the spot where Charlie was, but when I touch the sheet it isn't even warm. "Shit!" I sit up fast. "What time is it?"

"Time to hit the road. Roland doesn't know it yet, but he's driving us."

He sees me glance out the window. Sissy's brown bomber is still under the tree.

"Rhoda gave her a lift. So, you ready to roll?"

"Her car is dead, her roof is a couple of sheets of plastic, and you're going to skip on her?"

"Back off, Snowflake. Take a look at that sky." He gives me time to appreciate the cumulonimbus convention going on outside. "Not exactly roof weather, is it? So, here's the plan. I'll ride back to Tallahassee with you, pick up my things, be back here this afternoon. Whaddya say, are you up for it?"

"Are you kidding? I'm definitely up for it!" Maybe I can slide into lunch, watch Hofstra inhale his baloney. Sure it's gross, but I kind of miss it.

"Okay, then, chop-chop." He lopes down the stairs. I hear the front door slam. I pull a T-shirt over my head, then watch through the window as he thrashes into the scrub at the edge of the yard, cutting through to Roland's. We're getting out of here today, like, right now! Relief triggers a flood of adrenaline—and an instant stomachache. Hope I haven't missed too much.

Feeling for my shoes with my toes, I kick the stuffed rabbit that lies beside my bed. I pick it up and hold it in both hands. Charlie and I said goodbye last night, but after that I came back—he's beginning to think of me as the guy who says goodbye but never leaves. Sissy too. She expects me to be here when she comes home.

But maybe it's easier this way. I set the rabbit down on the bed and loop a pack strap over my shoulder. I really have to go.

As I come downstairs I see the crane Charlie and I built. It's lying on its side. I stand it up, but it still looks dinky. If I had the time, I'd tear it down and build him something to remember me by, something I put together dozens of times when I was an Erector-head: the mighty thunder lizard, T. rex. If I'd known about his fossils, that's what we would have built in the first place. It's too late now.

I drop my pack on the kitchen table and pour the last of the coffee into a mug. I add a few Mississippis of sugar and chug it. Funny, I arrive here having barely tasted coffee and leave an addict—I'll need plenty when I get home if I want to catch up. The knot in my stomach gets worse. I realize that twisted is its natural state whenever I think about the race to the Ivy League. Bright side? I had a couple days off and saw a little of the scenic side of Chiefland.

Still chewing the sugar, I rinse and dry the mug. When I open the cupboard to put it away, I see the tip jar. All that's left inside is a handful of nickels and dimes, a few pennies. I wonder how long it took her to get it to where it was yesterday. A week? A month? It isn't right. I make more tutoring.

I unzip the pouch in the front flap of my pack and pull out the wad of cash. I'm about to stuff all of it in the jar when I remember I'm dealing with Lonny, the living embodiment of Murphy's Law. Whatever can go wrong, will.

I keep two twenties and stuff the rest in the jar.

I think about writing a note. I don't want Lonny to get the credit. I pull Dad's index card out of the vocabulary book to write something on the back, but she'll know it's from me. For better or worse, I'm as close to a guardian angel as she has at the moment. I curl the card and pop it in the jar. The cupboard door closes with a click just as Lonny vaults into the kitchen. "Get it in gear, Snowflake. Roland'll be here in ten."

Roland's ten turns into twenty. While waiting, I run up to Charlie's room and bring down a few plastic soldiers. I'm posting them strategically around the crane—a little homeland security—when a horn blares out front. *Screee-ack.*

"Move your ass!" Lonny shouts from the kitchen. By the time my ass is in the kitchen, his is out the door. I stop long enough to collect my pack from the table and take one final look around.

Scree-ack-ack.

The door slams behind me. I jump from the porch to the ground.

Roland's truck pants, *huh, huh, huh.* Sounds as if he's dropped his muffler. The small guy behind the wheel hangs an arm out the window, his smile punctuated by half a dozen teeth, randomly distributed. "Hey, Fish, get in back." Lonny's already in the cab beside him.

"Why do I get the back?"

"You wanna go or not?" says Roland.

I follow my pack over the tailgate of the truck. Lonny drums the passenger door with the palm of the hand hanging out the window. Roland puts it into first.

As Roland jacks it into second, then third, it becomes clear that the muffler isn't the only thing Roland's lost. Shocks—what shocks? We wallop over the troughs in Sissy's driveway. When we reach the dirt road he hits the accelerator. Suddenly, we're doing sixty down the dirt road. I've never ridden in the back of a pickup before. Dad is a seatbelt kind of a guy. I wonder how dogs' ears stay attached when they ride in the back of an open pickup. The wind velocity is incredible.

Even though the rain has stopped, riding in the back of the Roland-mobile is damned cold. I dig my sweater out of my pack. It's damp and smells rank. I pull it over my head anyway—maybe it'll blow dry.

I'm halfway enjoying the sensation of rushing backwards when we pass Bett's Big T. Sissy is on break out front, a cigarette in her hand. Tired, her back is against the wall of the diner. She knows I have to leave—but I feel like I'm running out on her.

She's watching the ground when Roland hits the horn, *Skree-ack*. And we slow, just a little. "Taking the kid home," Lonny yells.

Wild-eyed, Sissy runs across the parking lot, trips, but catches herself on the hood of a parked truck. She shouts something, then stands at the edge of the road, fists clenched at her sides. She's still standing like that when she disappears behind a bend in the road. If she remembers me at all, she'll probably see me like this, sneaking off in the back of a truck. Some guardian angel. I didn't even wave.

I slump down until I'm lying in the truck bed. Numb, I watch the clouds tear past. The sky is unstable; it could rain any time. Lonny was right. He would have been crazy to take the tarp off this morning and get back to work. But Sissy didn't hear that discussion. She sees her roof crew taking off. And maybe that's what's happening. Lonny says he'll come back, but I'm not sure I believe him either.

To take my mind off Sissy, I make a mental list of the things I want to do when I get home: shower, eat a tuna sandwich, talk to Dez, put on dry underwear.... Imagining dry underwear, I fall asleep. I wake up when I slide and hit my head on the back of the cab. The truck has made an abrupt stop. I sit up long enough to see Lonny go into a liquor store, then I lie back down. I squint at my watch. We should be in Tallahassee in less than an hour. I hope that good old boy can keep the truck on the road while he and Lonny pass the bottle back and forth.

The truck tires crunch gravel and the sky rotates. Roland must have taken a detour to get to the liquor store and now we're backtracking. Seems as if I'm the only one in a rush to get to Tallahassee.

The tires thump over what has to be the ridge at the end of my driveway. I hear the brake ratchet. The engine idles. The front end of the truck is angled uphill—as it should be. Even the sky looks right. But when I sit up, the bump at the end of the driveway is someone else's bump; the driveway and the sky are someone else's too. We're parked in front of a small brick ranch house with three plastic ducks frozen in mid-waddle on the lawn.

Lonny stumbles out of the cab and kicks the nearest tire on the pickup parked in front of Roland's truck. He glares at the limp *Just Married* banner across the tailgate.

Roland hangs out the truck window. "Was I lyin'?"

Lonny stomps one of the *Congratulations!* Mylar balloons that drags on the ground.

"Lonny?" I kneel up in the bed of the truck. "Tell me we're in Tallahassee."

Roland holds his hand out the open window, palm up,

154

and waggles his fingers. "It's pay-up time." Lonny digs blindly in the pocket of his jeans and pulls out a few bills and some loose change, which he dumps in Roland's hand. "You're short," says Roland, counting it, "but close enough. Now how about we turn around and head for home?"

"Home?" I ask. "Whose home? I mean it, Lonny, where are we?"

But Lonny doesn't seem to hear either of us. He takes a couple of steps toward the house.

I stand up in the truck bed and pound the top of the cab. "Would *someone* tell me where we are?"

"Beautiful O-ca-la," sings Roland.

"Ocala! What the—! Why are we in Ocala?"

"We're visiting this bad boy's used-to-be best friend, Mike," says Roland. "Come on, Lonny, get back in. He's all growed up and married. He don't have time to play around with you."

Lonny returns to the truck only long enough to jerk his duffle bag out through the open cab window.

"You're on your own," says Roland. "I'm not sticking around for the fireworks."

I catch myself on the top of the cab as the truck begins to roll.

If I had time to think I'd realize that a ride back to Chiefland would be better than getting stranded in Ocala, but Roland is backing up fast. I grab my pack and jump. "Why are we here, Lonny? You said—"

"We're checking on my buddy, Mike Lopez. Funny he never told me he was getting married." He eyes a milk can beside the front door with daisies painted all over it. "Isn't that cute?" He throws his duffle bag down on the lawn, lopes up the two steps to the narrow concrete porch, and leans on the doorbell. Having waited patiently for half a second, he clubs the door with a fist.

"I don't believe this! You came all this way to beat up a guy who's not even here? What happened to taking me home?"

He rattles the knob, then steps back. "Hey, Mikey!" he bawls.

The door opens maybe six inches. In the gap I see a massive shoulder, one eye, half a black mustache. "Hey!" Lonny thumps himself on the chest with spread fingers. "Remember me?"

The door opens a little wider, and Mike slides out. Maybe because he's mostly bald, he looks older than Lonny. What hair he has is pulled into a ponytail. Mike resembles a WWF wrestler, but he's surprisingly gentle with the knob, turning it so it doesn't click when he closes the door. He grunts, "Hey!" then perpetrates the secret biker handshake on Lonny, but even as he does it he glances back at the door. "Lonny, what the hell brings you here?"

"I need a reason?"

"It's not the best time...." Mike passes a hand over his face and a blue snake, just like the one on Lonny's arm, sticks its head out below the cuff of Mike's sweatshirt.

I've got to get in this conversation and turn it some useful direction. "Mexico Mike, I presume?"

Mike looks from Lonny to me. "Who's the kid?"

"His name is Fish," says Lonny.

"Shouldn't he be in school?" Mike asks.

I say, "Yeah, I should, and I would, except this dumb-ass—"

"Since when have you worried about school, Mike?" Lonny cuts me off. "Now, are you going to invite me in—like you invited me to the wedding?"

Mike pushes his tongue against the inside of his cheek, then makes a weak excuse about how he didn't know how to get in touch. "You move around, you know?"

"Sissy always manages to find me."

Mike clears his throat. "Carla thought it'd be better if you didn't come."

"Carla? I'm your goddamn best friend."

"Hell, man, it was her wedding. Girl stuff, ya know? All I did was rent the tux and show up at the church. Figured you wouldn't want to come anyway."

"Congratulations," I say, pacing back and forth at the foot of the steps. "Now, can someone figure out how I'm going to get home?"

Lonny flicks Mike's wedding band with his forefinger. "Sure you shouldn't wear this in your nose?" He swings around and gives the milk can a savage kick. It smashes into the wall and bounces back. Lonny's second kick sends it into the yard where it bowls over Mama duck, pulling the little wires in her feet right out of the dirt. "What exactly is that woman's problem?" he pants.

Mike puts a hand on Lonny's shoulder. "Now, don't go nuts on me, but she doesn't want you in her house," he says. "Not after the last time."

Lonny knocks Mike's hand off his shoulder. "What do you mean, the last time? Sure, I was drunk, but you were too!"

"As a skunk," Mike says, grinning. For a second I see the old Mike bob to the surface. But in a heartbeat that Mike submerges again. "Find yourself a place to crash, okay? I'll come by later." He glances at the door again. "Right after Bible study."

I try to picture a map of Florida, wondering if forty bucks will get me home from Ocala.

"Bible study?" Lonny snorts.

"Just tell me where you're going to be," says Mike. "There must be somebody you guys can crash with. Stony? Rich?"

"Bible study?" Lonny repeats.

"How 'bout Les?" Mike suggests.

Lonny crosses his arms. "We're staying right here with you, blood."

"Sorry, compadre, no can do." Mike pulls a ring of keys out of his pocket and gives it a cheerful shake. "Looks like it's cheap motel time. I'll drive ya."

"Drop me at the Greyhound station," I say.

Mike turns toward me briefly—I was beginning to think I was invisible. "I can do that," he says.

But Lonny holds up a hand. "Forget it, Mikey. We wouldn't want to make you late for *Bible* study." He stalks down the steps and throws the duffle bag strap over his shoulder. "Write this down, Fish. Some guys'll do anything to get in a girl's pants."

Mike's chest swells, his chin juts. "Don't you talk about Carla like that, and don't mock the Lord, Lonny."

"I'm not talking about Carla, and Jesus and me get along just fine." He whips around and points a finger at Mike, televangelist style. "I'm talking about *you,* man! *You!* Come on, Fish. Let's get out of here."

But I stay put. "I need that ride to the bus, Mike. Can you help me out?"

Mike moves me aside with one hand. "You want some cash, Lonny?" he calls, making one last attempt, but Lonny never slows.

Mike stares at the back of Lonny's head. "Screw you!" His full strength goes into opening the door—I expect it to fly off the hinges. But then he must remember Carla, wedding bells, turning the other cheek, because he closes the door behind him softly.

"About that ride...." I say to the closed door.

"Who was that guy?" Lonny mutters. "Not Mike Lopez. He hasn't been Mike Lopez since Carla Hyle got ahold of him. The Mike I knew was like a brother."

"Listen, Lonny—I don't have time for this. Where are we going?" We've been walking for twenty minutes, fast, but all this hustle seems like a way to blow off steam, not get somewhere.

Lonny hangs a right on a street called Magnolia. He

walks up to a building with a sign that says Able Body. It's a place that hires day laborers. "This is my stop," he says.

"What about Sissy's roof?"

"Knock it off about the roof, okay? I gotta pick up a couple days work, resuscitate the old cash reserve." He shades his eyes and peers through the glass.

I stare at his back. He's blown Sissy and Charlie off. And he's blowing me off too. "You happen to know where the bus station is?" I say.

"Any closer, it would bite ya."

Across the street is an old-time brick train station, but the building must be doing double duty, because over one door is the unmistakable silhouette of The Dog.

"Yes!" I yell, raising both arms. "There is a god!"

"You and Mike," he says, shaking his head.

The clouds over the station are like dirigibles filled with water, ready to dump their loads. I hope the sky is different over Sissy's house—but all of a sudden Chiefland is shrinking, flattening. Soon it will be a postcard: where I went on my personal spring break. I'll miss Charlie and Sissy—and I want to miss them—but missing them will be churned under by the effort to catch up with my real life.

The feebly blinking sign over the ticket counter proclaims "Peace On Earth." It's not exactly the season, but time seems to be standing still in this room. A young guy sleeps with his feet propped on a battered guitar case. A grandmotherly woman sits with two children sleeping against her. One drools on her sleeve. Sissy asked where you go to give up. This might be the place.

"May I help you?" The elderly black man behind the counter wears a badge that reads *Avery*. There's no indication whether it's a first or last name. He looks at me over his glasses, his nose wrinkling as he catches a whiff of the smell emanating from my damp pack. He doesn't comment except to ask, "Destination?"

"Tallahassee."

"One way or round trip?"

"One way."

He nods, like that's about what he expected. "There's a five twenty-seven. It'll get you into Tally at ten sharp."

It's later than I'd hoped, but not bad. The bus station might not be totally night-of-the-living-dead at ten.

"That'll be thirty-eight dollars."

I congratulate myself on keeping those forty bucks. "You got it!" I say, louder than I mean to. The guy with the guitar case twitches, then tries to dig a shoulder into the plastic bench. The woman with the two children puts her finger to her lips.

"Sorry." I unzip the front pocket of my pack. When I reach inside for the cash I feel slick nylon, nothing else. As I move my fingers around in the small pouch I glance up. "It was in here this morning!" The clerk's brown eyes are sympathetic, but not surprised. "Just a sec," I say, and I drop the pack on the floor. I squat beside it and pry the pouch open as wide as it will go. The fingers didn't lie. It's empty.

"I must have stuffed it somewhere else." I jump to my

feet, check my pockets, then fall back to a squat and grab the tab and rip the zipper on the body of the pack open. When I dump everything on the floor, something dark clatters across the brick tile and skids to a stop against the base of the ticket counter. Charlie's sloth toenail—his prize fossil. I pick it up and hold it in my hand.

"Will you be wanting that ticket?" All I see over the edge of the counter are Avery's eyes.

"Just a second." I kneel up and put the fossil in my pocket, then shake out each piece of sweaty scrunched-up clothes, twice. Giving Lonny what Dad calls the benefit of the doubt, I even open the plastic bags of wet clothes. The bad-breath stench of anaerobic bacteria almost knocks me over, but the money's not in there. I beat my fists against the pile. "God-damn, goddamn, goddamn! The goddamn son of a bitch robbed me!"

Chair legs scrape the floor as Avery pulls himself up to his full height—somewhere around five-foot-five. "You'd better take that language outside, son."

I blink up at him. "I'm sorry, Mr. Avery."

"Don't apologize to me; apologize to that woman and her two little children."

"Sorry. I don't usually shout curse words in public places, but I'm dangerously close to the edge here. If I'm not in school tomorrow, I'll have three unexcused absences. If I miss one more day after that I'll zero the semester."

No one responds. I stare at my hands resting on the knees of my filthy jeans. There's dirt under the nails, and the dent on my left middle finger, the supposedly permanent trough made by a pen pressing against it, is gone. The guy with the 4.80 GPA is flickering as bad as the "Peace on Earth" sign above the counter. The stony silence in the room says, tough. My story is nothing compared to the stories that come through this station every day.

The thing is, it's the only one I've got.

I stand up slowly, keeping my knees bent—small guys don't like it when you tower over them—and I throw myself on the mercy of Greyhound. "I've been traveling with a friend...well, he seemed like a friend. I had forty dollars, I swear. He took it out of my pack—"

"Should have kept it in your pocket," says the guy with the guitar, never opening his eyes.

"I should have, I know," I agree. I turn back to Mr. Avery. "But I didn't, and I *have* to get home. I mean, have to. Is there any way I could ride now, pay later, like as soon as I get home?"

Avery is shaking his head like a dashboard bobble-head. "I can take a credit card; I can take cash. With two forms of ID I can take a personal check. But Greyhound doesn't have any ride-now-pay-later plan." He nods at a yellow and black sign behind the counter. "Can you get someone to wire you the money Western Union?"

"There *isn't* anyone. But maybe you, I mean maybe you personally—"

The head shaking gets worse. "Don't even ask, son. You'll just embarrass both of us."

I turn toward the other riders. "Is there a good Samaritan in the house?" I ask, desperate. The guitar guy pretends

163

he's asleep again. The woman looks at me with empty eyes. There isn't a bit of compassion there—or anything else. She's just waiting for a bus, two small children drooling on her. The suitcase between her feet is a paper shopping bag with string handles. She can't afford compassion.

"Sorry," I say to the room in general. "Sorry." I stuff everything in the pack as fast as I can and turn to slink out, just as Lonny pushes the door open.

"Ya get your ticket?"

The woman on the bench and the guitar player—suddenly wide awake—shift so they can watch the action. "This your friend?" asks Mr. Avery.

I stride over and grab the front of Lonny's shirt with both hands. "Did I get a ticket? You *know* I didn't."

"And why didn't you?"

"You robbed me, that's why. I want my money!"

"I didn't rob you," Lonny insists.

"Then where's his forty bucks?" the woman asks.

"Yeah!" I twist the fabric in my hands. "Don't tell me you didn't take it out of my pack."

"Of course I did." He locks onto my wrists and squeezes. Just before the pain drops me to my knees I let go. "I had to pay Roland for driving you home, didn't I?"

I spread my arms. "Does this look like home?"

"So, there was a slight change of plans. But what's forty bucks? I saw the wad of cash you were carrying."

I realize that after paying Roland and buying booze he's broke too. Whatever can go wrong, will.

He pushes me toward the counter. "Do it, Snowflake, dig

out the cash and pay the man. It's time for you to go home."

"I don't have it any more, okay?"

"What the hell?" Lonny looks genuinely surprised. "I've been with you every second. You didn't go nowhere you could spend it…." He stares at me. I stare back. One corner of his mouth twists up. "Don't tell me. She sweet-talked it out of you."

"She doesn't even know about it. I left it in her tip jar."

"Well, how about that?" he says softly. "Sissy Erle has herself a knight in shining armor."

"She and Charlie need *somebody*—you sure haven't been much help."

His jaws tighten, and I think, *oh, shit*. I've seen him like this. This is the Lonny who launches Erector sets and knocks over ducks. I raise my fists, but as I do, he falls onto one of the benches. Throwing his legs out straight, he starts to laugh.

I glare at him between my fists. "What's so funny?"

"You! You robbed yourself, Mr. White Knight." He wipes his eyes with the back of his wrist. "Looks like you're going to have to get that ticket money the old-fashioned way, trade a day of sweat for it."

"But I don't have a day! If I miss school tomorrow I'm screwed!"

"Yeah? That's life. Get used to it." He stands up and puts a hand on my back. "Come on across the street, Fish. Let me introduce you to my new friend, Mr. Huston. Tomorrow you and me are going to paint us a house."

9

onny has to do some fast-talking to convince the man at Able Body that I'm not a runaway, not skipping school, that I'm older than I look. "I'm short a couple boys," he finally says, to let Lonny know he doesn't believe him but can't afford not to. "Be here at seven, sharp." And *boom*, I'm a housepainter.

"Unexcused absence number three." I say as we walk away. "Unbelievable. And what are we supposed to do until we paint that house? Where do we sleep? What do we eat?"

"I'm working on it." His shoulders are hunched, his hands in his pockets. It isn't raining but the air is damp. So are our clothes. Cold infiltrates our pores.

For a while we try walking into stores. We act like we need hardware, books, anything so we can warm up. But we can't stay long. The way we look makes everyone but Greyhound riders nervous.

We beat a hasty retreat from a home furnishing store where we've been lurking among the living room suites when an "associate"offers to assist us. "My hands didn't even have time to defrost," I complain. "Any other great ideas?"

"Can't think," he says. "I'm freezing my ass off."

"My ass is history too. But let's review. We've already established that you've blown all the money you stole from me. We get about five minutes in any store before the manager hits the silent alarm button. This isn't working and I need to get home, like, right now." Suddenly blinding inspiration strikes. "Hey, how about if we hitch?"

He stops dead on the sidewalk. "Do you know how bad you look, Snowflake?"

"No worse than you," I say, stopping beside him.

"Don't bet on it." He slaps his arms vigorously.

"I hope that helps, because you look like a spastic chicken."

"Don't mention food," he says. "Come on, let's go."

"Where?" I demand. "I'm not going until you tell me where." But just then the sky opens up. The rain comes down so hard it hurts.

"Aw, crap!" Lonny yelps. He whirls around, sizing up our get-out-of-the-rain prospects. The curly letters on the plate glass window beside us announce: Sister Rita, Reader Advisor. He jerks Sister Rita's door open and we dive into a narrow hallway with carpet the color of snot.

"We could just stay here by the door," I whisper. We'll be invited to leave as soon as the psychic takes one look at us.

"I want heat," he says, heading for the bead curtain at the end of the hall.

"Sister Rita will be real glad to see us," I mumble. Sneakers squishing, I follow him into a room draped with Indian bedspreads—enough to supply a decent-sized Pier 1. The lighting is dim—one bare low-watt bulb and a few candles. A giant eye is painted on the far wall.

Seated on a couch below the eye, chowing down on what looks like a sausage and onion sandwich, is a girl wearing a paisley head scarf. Sister Rita, I presume. She takes a quick swig from a can of Diet Mountain Dew and swallows. "Are you two gentlemen seeking guidance?" The voice is probably an octave lower than her real one; she looks young.

"Who isn't?" Lonny falls into the overstuffed chair opposite the couch. He eyes the paper plate in her lap. Under the mumbo-jumbo of jasmine and patchouli incense, we both smell the food. I wonder if anyone's ever committed aggravated assault to get their hands on a half-eaten sausage sandwich. She tucks the paper plate under the coffee table and delicately wipes her fingers on her flowered skirt. "Are you here for a reading?"

"Depends on how much it costs," says Lonny.

I fall into a second duct-taped lounge chair. I don't know what hustle Lonny's running. Since we don't have any money, cost is irrelevant. But I'll soak up the warmth while I can.

Under the goth makeup—white powder and heavy black eyeliner—Sister Rita looks scared. She glances back and forth between us, but nothing she sees reassures her. "Ten dollars a reading?" she suggests timidly.

"Ten bucks?" Lonny looks over his left shoulder, then his right. "I don't see a line. How about if we give you fifteen for the both of us?"

This is great. He doesn't have fifteen dollars; he doesn't have fifteen cents. Still, he's bargaining.

Sister Rita bites her lip and glances toward a second bead curtain at the back of the room. When nothing happens she shrugs, the bangles on her arms clinking softly. "Okay," she says. "Fifteen." Then she asks Lonny to hold out his hand. "You are a seeker…" she begins.

While she peers into Lonny's future, I put the chair back and study a water stain on the ceiling. It looks like a specimen of *Fucus serratus* algae—which makes me think about Leon and its boring labs, its droning teachers.

God, I wish I were there.

I close my eyes to the soothing sound of Sister Rita's voice. She should probably be in school too. Bet math did her in. I wonder if she'd be any easier to tutor than Annie. My arm drops like a dead weight off the arm of the chair, jolting me awake. I force myself to listen to the palm reader's words. I've never been to an actual reading before, but Lonny's seems pretty standard—or else Sister Rita and I have been watching the same movies and TV shows. You will take a long trip; you should beware of a dark-haired man who wishes you harm. At that news, he grins over at me. "Sounds like you, Fish."

"She's right about that." I flex my icy fingers and try to absorb the heat in the room.

In a nod to his dirty clothes and soaked boots she adds, "Better days are ahead." The whole reading takes five minutes by my watch—which works out to ninety bucks an hour. Not bad.

"Now you," she says. "Give me your hand, the one you write with."

I pop the chair back into the upright-and-locked position. Then, as an experiment, I hold out the right one, but she won't take it. "The one you write with," she repeats. I give her my left hand. First she examines my fingers. I'm embarrassed by the dirt under the nails. "Long and tapered," she says, "like your mother's." I feel a small shiver run down my spine. "They indicate an artistic temperament."

Sister Rita turns my hand over. I wait for her to tell me I'll go on a long journey or acquire sudden wealth. Instead, a scared, sobbing sound comes from the back of her throat. Lonny rolls his eyes.

"Lost," she moans. "Something or someone important to you is lost. I see a man grieving...."

I slide to the edge of the chair. My knees knock against hers. "My dad!"

"Yes, yes! Your father is weeping for you." Her eyes shine with tears as she stares into mine. "But he is not the one who is lost. The one who is lost is a woman. I see a river with no way across."

"No way across for who? Her or me?"

"No way across," she repeats, blinking back tears that look real.

"But—what should I do?"

Just then, Lonny stands up and stretches. "Thanks for the cosmic connection, Rita, but we gotta go."

"Wait!" I sputter. She knows something important!

Lonny grabs the back of my sweater and jacks me to my feet.

"You owe me fifteen dollars," says the girl in a high, whiny voice. "We agreed."

Lonny and I are on our way to the door when she sounds the alarm. "Mom! Couple of deadbeats in here." A Sister Rita double—only super-sized—bursts through the second bead curtain waving a spatula. They look like a couple of nesting babushka dolls—the mother is the big fat outside doll, the daughter one of the smaller inside ones.

The bell on the door jangles when Lonny wrenches it open. Big Babushka is panting right behind me. A fist locks onto my sweater, but I twist out of her grip and take off, following Lonny as he sprints through the puddles. If only Coach Dickerson could see me now.

We pant, our backs against a graffiti-scarred wall blocks away from Sister Rita's psychic parlor. "Hoo-wee!" exclaims Lonny. "That was close!"

Rain is falling so hard I can feel it bouncing off my scalp. "How'd she know all that stuff?" I gasp.

"Exactly what stuff did she know?"

"About my missing mom, and my father grieving over me—he will if he gets home and I'm not there."

"How'd she know?" He shakes his wet hair out of his eyes. "Could it be because she's so psychic? Nah. Could it be because you told her? Bingo."

"I didn't tell her!"

"Sure you did. She said 'a man,' you said 'Dad.' She jumped right on it."

"But still—"

"It's the way they work, Snowflake. She threw things out until you rang like a slot machine spitting quarters, and you went for it. She's a first-class fake."

"What does that make you? She did her job and you didn't pay her."

"You knew I wasn't going to when you parked your butt on her Barcalounger." He tries to light up but the wet cigarette droops, the lighter sputters. "She should have known too, being psychic and all. Besides, what did we cheat her out of? Words. Just wish I could have scored that sandwich…."

"I would have fought you for it." Water is running down my eyeglass lenses. I don't have a single thing that is dry enough to wipe them with. "What did we get out of that little encounter? We warmed up for fifteen minutes, cheated Sister Rita, now we're back on the street. We need something more permanent. Try this: Call your brother. Have him send some money Western Union—"

"Try this," he shoots back. "Call your dad. You're the one who's in trouble."

I lean my pack against the wall under an awning that says Leitner's Pharmacy. Lonny drops his duffle. It's twilight. We've been walking for hours through a slow drizzle, sheltering in doorways when we can, moving from one semi-dry spot to the next. Now we peer over stacked boxes of cold medications in the front window, spying on the silver-haired man behind the counter. "That's him," Lonny says. "Old man Leitner. I worked for the guy when I was in high school."

"Does that mean we can go in and warm up?"

"Wait out here, Fish. Let me talk to him. I only worked a couple months, but who knows. Maybe he'll let us crash in the storeroom or something—it'd beat camping."

"Tell me you were the model employee."

He slicks his wet hair back with his hands. "Shit. By now he's probably forgotten why he fired me, right? It's been a few."

"Why *did* he fire you, Lonny?"

But he's already in the door, striding toward the counter. I know his wet boots are making disgusting sucking sounds, but he acts like he owns the place. Mr. Leitner glances up. He shrinks a little like he expects to be robbed. I shift to one side so I can see around the Theraflu boxes.

Lonny starts talking, explaining who he is: that kid who worked for you, like, six years ago, remember? He laughs. Bet he made a joke about getting fired. The old guy isn't laughing, but I can tell he recognizes Lonny. He says something back, but he still doesn't smile. Lonny laughs some more and puts a hand on the old guy's arm. Mr. Leitner glances over his shoulder like he's looking for backup.

Not a promising start, but Lonny keeps talking. Maybe he can convince Leitner to let us sleep on the pharmacy floor. I catch myself getting excited about sleeping on linoleum. Pitiful, but it's the best I can expect if I leave things up to Lonny.

I feel for the phone card in my pocket. I have to call someone for help—not Dad, but somebody. I look around and—like it's meant to be—there's a pay phone in front of the store next door. It wasn't there before, I swear.

I'm so cold my hand shakes as I punch in the nine zillion numbers on the card—I can hardly read them in the dim light. A cheerful, electronically generated voice tells me to press one for English, press two for—

I press one. The same voice informs me there is an additional ten-minute charge for calls made from a pay phone.

"Usury!" I shout. I'm enraged.

The voice goes on unperturbed. "You have twenty-five minutes of call time remaining on your card. You may dial the desired number now."

I dial Hofstra—Hofstra has a car—then drum my fingers on the glass door while the phone rings.

"Hello?" Minor setback. It's his mother.

"Good evening, Mrs. Hofstra. This is Fisher. May I please speak to Gregory?"

"Sorry, Fisher. Gregory's phone privileges have been revoked. We caught him drinking." She says it like she's sure I know all about the drinking.

"Please, Mrs. Hofstra. I need to speak to him. I don't want to break your rules or anything, but this is a major emergency!"

"Are you bleeding, Fisher?"

"No, but—"

She hangs up on me. She probably thinks I'm an accomplice in Hofstra's drinking. I'm not. In fact, I'm kind of glad they caught him; maybe they'll straighten him out. But that burned up critical time on the card.

I have just enough left for one call. One. I dial Raleigh's, but hang up fast. "Shit," I whisper. I rest my forehead on the glass, breathing hard. Raleigh's car is in the shop.

Dez.

She might be able to borrow the Vic and come get me. No, even Boots has enough maternal instincts to know that driving to Ocala in the unreliable Vic is a bad idea.

That leaves Dad—I've been so afraid to tell him, but maybe he owes me. Becoming an achiever wasn't my idea. I was having a good time back in sixth cutting up with Ramos. Dad and I are in this together. My success is his success. Nobody's perfect all the time; he knows that better than anyone. And I came damn close.

So here's what's going to happen. I'll call. He'll Western Union the money to Avery—maybe there's a bus in the middle of the night I can get on. I'll look like the last guy on *Survivor* when I drag myself into school. I won't be alert. I may not even be awake but—bottom line—I'll be there. The damage will be limited to two unexcused absences. Academic perfection will resume, no harm done. Dad *has* to help me.

I dial the card number again, punch one for English. My hand isn't shaking any more. I hit the buttons hard. "Come on, come on…" But the robot voice is not done chatting. "You can add additional time for just five cents a minute at Wal-Mart." Then the voice encourages me to press one to find out about the "automatic dialing feature."

When I don't press anything the canned voice reminds me, "There is an additional ten-minute charge for calls made from a pay phone. Your card has fourteen minutes of call time remaining."

Fourteen minus ten leaves four.

I have four minutes to tell Dad what's happening and what he needs to do about it. The electronic voice chirps, "Dialing!" And the tune that is Nana's number plays in my ear. It rings five times—which scares me to death—then Dad picks up. "Hello?"

"Dad, hi, it's me."

"Fisher! Great to hear your voice, son." His voice sounds thin and old.

"What's the matter, Dad?" Damn, it's no time to be checking on his mental health.

He sighs. "I just came across some photos of you, me, and Mom in Nana's desk."

Why now? He never talks about Mom. Why now?

"We've done all right, though, haven't we?" he goes on. "You and me, we've stayed the course."

"I guess…" I watch two raindrops race each other down

the glass, moving as fast as the passing seconds. "But listen, Dad—"

"I'm very lucky to have a son like you. So many of the kids I counsel are going nowhere. You have a good head on your shoulders, you work hard. You know where you're going and what it takes to get there."

Go ahead, Dad. Lay it on thick. Drown me.

"What did you fix yourself for supper?" he asks, ping-ponging to the next pointless subject.

My empty stomach ties itself in a knot. "Chicken stew and salad."

He says he's proud of me for doing such a good job taking care of myself while he's away.

I feel about five years old. Before hanging up I have to promise not to study too hard—that'll be easy. He tells me to give his best to Desiree. I say "sure thing" and hang up before an electronic woman lets him know that his responsible son is calling on a phone card that has just expired.

I open the phone booth door and hurl the calling card like a throwing star—but it's just a crappy piece of plastic. Instead of blazing an arc to the nearest storefront and burying a point or two in the wood, it lands in a puddle, like, two feet away.

And I pick it up. Screwed on every front, I still can't litter; Dad's training is hard-wired.

As I jam the card back in my pocket, the door of Leitner's smacks the wall. Lonny swings the duffle over his shoulder and walks away.

I scramble to get my pack. "Let me guess. Mr. Leitner remembered?"

"Oh, yeah. In detail."

"This is it," says Lonny, stepping over the metal rail at the edge of the road, "The Last Chance Motel."

"Where?" I don't see a motel. To me it looks like the only thing we're doing is abandoning the pavement for wet grass—which is not an improvement, but maybe I'm missing something. It's dark and I'm having a hard time seeing anything through the rain on my glasses.

Lonny shoe-skates down a steep embankment. I quickly lose sight of him. "Come on down, Fish." His voice, which has taken on a hollow echo, comes from somewhere far below.

I slide after him, afraid I'll land on my butt. I'm still on my feet when I hit level ground. Now the voice comes from above. "Up here, Fish!"

"What the…?" I take a couple of steps toward the sound of his voice and the rain stops.

I'm under something. A bridge? I can't tell for sure. The air smells like drowned campfire. To my left are what might be houses. They're not that close and through the drops on my lenses their lights are rainbowed fractals.

I wipe my glasses on my wet shirtfront, put them back on my face, and look up, and yes, that's definitely a bridge up there. "How high up is it?" I shout to Lonny. The tires of the cars passing overhead sound pretty far away.

"Forty, fifty feet." His voice echoes. As my eyes adjust to the dark I see the steep concrete ramps that support the bridge. They phosphoresce in the low light. Running down the middle of the flat, sandy stretch between the ramps is the gleam of a railroad track.

"Come on up," Lonny shouts.

Aping along on all fours, I climb the ramp toward the sound of his voice.

Somewhere above me I hear him unzip his bag, then a click. Suddenly I can see the pattern of the small blood vessels in my retinas. "Jeez, can you aim that thing some other way?"

He points the flashlight up. In the bounce light from the concrete overhead I see the calves of his jeans, his boots. Lonny is sitting on a sort of ledge where the bridge meets the ground. I clamber up and sit beside him. "Smells like piss up here."

"At least it's dry," he counters. The ledge we're sitting on is about six feet wide and runs the width of the bridge like a shelf.

Lonny shines the light both ways along the ledge. A few beer bottles wink back—we're not the first to hole up here—but that's not what he's looking for. "Good," he says. "The motel's empty." He directs the beam at the ledge at the top of the ramp on the other side of the bridge. The light is almost too feeble to travel that far. Through smeared glasses, I can't even see what's over there, but Lonny seems satisfied.

He directs the light up at the underside of the bridge.

"Check this out." As he plays the beam across the concrete, painted messages appear briefly, then dematerialize. I pull my shirt out of my jeans. With my last dry square inch of clothing, I wipe my glasses and read:

Josh 'n Tiffany
The Class of '99 Rocks!
Go Bulldogs!

The light beam skips from message to message. "Must've painted over it," he says. The light doubles back, then stops on a lopsided heart: *L.T. + L.T.* "Still there!" he hoots.

"Lonny Traynor loves Lonny Traynor?"

The beam highlights the top pair of initials. "Lonny Traynor." It bounces to the second one. "Lisa Toricelli."

Maybe Lisa Toricelli is the Annie Cagney of Lonny's past. The girl who didn't know he was alive. Maybe there's something we both failed at. "Tell me about her."

"About who? Lisa? What's to tell? I sat up here with Mike, a can of spray paint, and a bottle of Mad Dog. One thing led to another…." He shakes his head. "Lisa Toricelli. She was one ugly chick."

"She was ugly, but you liked her?"

"Liked her? You gotta be shittin' me." He balances the flashlight on its end—which is when I realize it's the flashlight out of Sissy's car. He struggles to light a damp cigarette. "That was the year of the dare."

"The what?"

"Mike and me, we were sophomores, bored stupid, so we

started daring each other. It started out small. We had this decrepitated Spanish teacher, Señora Jones."

"Thought you didn't learn Spanish in school."

"Hell, she couldn't speak Spanish. Anyway, Mike dared me to steal a hairpin. I did it. She never felt a thing. I dared him to put it back. He stabbed her in the head. Got him in mucho hot water."

"Sounds pretty lame."

"Of course it was lame. School is lame. Like I said, we were bored." Lonny falls back on his hands and stares at the heart. "Mike got me good with this one though," he says, talking around the cigarette. "I paint it and think, the dare's done, right? Then Mike walks Lisa up here. After that she wouldn't leave me alone. I invited her to a dance, then stood her up. It was the only way to cure her."

"*That* was cold."

"Yeah? Life is cold." And I think of the dance Dez wanted me to take her to. He picks up a bottle cap and flips it. We listen to it click as it bounces down the ramp. "Word of advice: never stand up an ugly girl. Lisa slashed a couple tires. Problem was, it was my dad's truck. He took his belt off for that one. See down there?" Lonny points toward what I thought were houses. Through relatively clean glasses I can see a trailer park behind a chain-link fence. "I used to live there with my dad back in the day, Mike too—plus the lovely Lisa Toricelli."

"Is your dad still there?" Lonny probably screwed him over, but it's worth asking. It's really cold under this bridge.

"Nah. He croaked."

"Too bad. Guess that means we can't crash with him." I think about what I just said. "Sorry, Lonny. That's rough."

"Yeah. Jimmy was a harmless old guy, at least when he kept his belt on." He picks up the flashlight and casually clicks it off. "Found him dead one morning."

"God, Lonny!"

The lit end of his cigarette bobs with each word. "I closed his eyes and sat with him until I saw Mike's mom through the window of their trailer, parading around in her slip." He takes a deep drag and the small fire brightens. I can see his lips, the turned-down corners of his mouth. "She called 911, but there wasn't any rush. Jimmy wasn't going anywhere." He jettisons the cigarette butt. "Last one," he says as the butt hits the ramp and rolls, trailing sparks.

"Was your brother there?"

"Dave? Dave booked as soon as the Army would take him. I was six when he left."

"Where was your mother?"

I hear a dry laugh. "Same place as yours. Long as I can remember there was no one around but the old man. Even before he croaked, I was pretty much on my own. Most of the time it was just Mike and me. The two of us stood up on this bridge and tossed Jimmy's ashes into the wind. *Hasta la vista.* After that little ceremony I traded the trailer for a VW camper with a full tank of gas and got out of Dodge. I went up to Chiefland for a while, stayed with my aunt and uncle, but they wanted to tell me when to eat and when to breathe and when to swallow my spit. I stayed long enough to hook up with Sissy…but you know that story."

183

Click. The light comes back on and Lonny reaches into his duffle. "Put on anything dry you have. It'll be cold enough to freeze your nuts tonight."

I find a T-shirt and pull it on over my sweater, adding another thin layer. I dig out an extra pair of socks that's dirty but almost dry, and switch them out with the wet ones on my feet—then plug my feet back into the same wet sneakers.

Lonny tugs a second T-shirt over his head too. Before pulling it down like a cocoon he reaches out and turns off the light. "Good night, John Boy." We both stretch out on the ledge.

We need down sleeping bags and all we have is a couple of T-shirts. Our nuts are in deep trouble. But Lonny's not worried. In about a minute his breathing gets loud and slow. The man can fall asleep anywhere.

I listen to tires cross the bridge. Lying on damp concrete is like swimming in cold water. I can practically feel my core temperature drop. I can just see the headline: National Merit Finalist Found Frozen Under Bridge.

Which is the least of my worries. Tomorrow is the third unexcused absence. The last I can possibly get away with. I have to get home. If I work a day, it shouldn't be hard, but with Lonny in the equation, I don't know. Everything with Lonny is completely non-linear; it's Random Walk all the way.

A train clangs under the bridge. It rattles my bones but Lonny sleeps through it. I guess living in a trailer by the tracks has made him immune.

What finally wakes him up is nowhere near as loud as the train.

He snorts, then flops onto his back. "What the hell is that racket?"

"My t-teeth. I'm fr-fr-freezing."

"You need to take your mind off of it."

"Eating would take my m...mind off it."

"Tomorrow we'll work for Able Body, then get ourselves a big old supper. How does steak sound?"

It's not going to happen; I'll be on the bus by then. Still, I can almost smell that steak. "I'll take mine with onion rings." I swallow a mouthful of saliva.

"And rolls, mashed potatoes, gravy."

"And p-pie." I can't take it. I almost break down over pie.

Something hard presses my chest. "Have a swig."

I sit up and grab the flat bottle. My hand's so cold it's hard to hold on. "W-what's this?"

"It's what the doctor ordered."

The liquid burns its way down my esophagus. It slams my empty stomach, but I feel an instant warm sensation in my gut. "Decent!" I pass it back.

We take a few more hits off the bottle, passing it back and forth. The fireball never leaves my stomach. My arms and legs, my face, are still freezing. I stare into the dark, trying to remember the word for getting dangerously cold. I push things around inside my head, hunting for it.

The edge of the bottle presses my arm. "Go ahead, Fish. Kill it."

As I swallow the last mouthful of lightning, the word I've been looking for floats to the top of my brain like the answer in a Magic 8-Ball. "Hypoth-th-thermia. I th-think I've g-got it."

"Hypothermia? That means freezing your ass off, right?"

"R-right." My autonomic functions seem to be slowing down. The brain dies last. I read that somewhere—or maybe it was in a Steve Martin film. *The Man With Two Brains.* Good movie.

To prevent brain death I pick the word up, take it apart. *Hypo-,* meaning "less than." *Thermia,* meaning "heat," as in thermal, thermometer, thermos, thermocline. Hypothermia: less than heat. That's me. Totally less than heat.

"Fish? You losing it, man?"

"S-sorry." A creaky, demonic cackle is circling like a bat under the bridge. I didn't even know I was laughing.

"What's so funny anyway?"

"N-nothing." I can't tell him I was laughing at a word. Lonny's brain doesn't work that way—even when he's not freezing his ass off.

"Tell you what we're gonna do," he says. "We'll play us a little game. I guarantee you'll forget all about being cold."

Even though I can't see him, I cut my eyes his way. "What k-kind of game?"

He doesn't say the word loud, but it echoes eerily. "Dare."

"Like you and Mike did the year of the dare?"

"Why not? It passes the time."

The booze hasn't warmed my extremities, but it's done

something. I feel detached, yet strangely lucid. I understand it's going to be me who has to do whatever stupid, risky thing Lonny has in mind, but what the hell. I've got to have a few kick-ass stories to tell about being sixteen, and this is my last night of living dangerously. Tomorrow night I'll be chained to my desk; the biggest danger will be eyestrain. "O-k-kay. Let's d-do it."

"I'm too old to do crap like this," I tell him, beginning to hyperventilate.

He puts his knuckles on his hips. "Too old, or too chicken shit?"

Lonny's dare is the kind of thing a buddy could talk you into at, say, age ten. If it went okay you'd tell your own kids about it—as a warning. If it went wrong it would get you killed. Then other parents would use *you* as a warning.

"Pick something else, Lonny."

"What are you scared of?" he says, leaning over the bridge railing. "I don't see a thing." In contrast with the well-lit bridge, the ground below is in total darkness.

"It's down there though. Terra firma. Terra *very* firma."

He steps up onto the railing. "It's easy. See?"

"Get down, Lonny, you're drunk!"

"You too," he says, wobbling.

"Not enough to try that."

He sways out over the void and spits. I imagine that spit gob falling for miles.

My tongue feels thick. And some part of my numbed brain knows what I'm going to say is preachy. I say it anyway. "Let me point out the obvious. This is dangerous."

"So?" He swings a leg and pivots. Now his boots are lined up heel to toe on the edge of the barrier. He takes a couple of steps, and a pair of disembodied headlights appears in the distance.

The car passes, horn blaring. A wet wind sideswipes us. "Get down, Lonny, you proved your point." The *P*s come out with a popping sound. Some of whatever we were drinking has made it across the blood-brain barrier. The mouth is misfiring.

"Haven't proved a thing," he says. "Not until I go aaa-ll the way."

"Define aaa-ll the way."

"From metal to metal." That's when I notice that the ramps leading to the bridge are bordered by short metal guardrails, but on the bridge itself, the barricades are cement. "If it's concrete I'm walkin' it," he declares.

I stride the length of the bridge, then stop. "It's impossible," I shout back at him. "It's more than fifty yards. It can't be done."

"What do you mean, can't be done?" He skips a couple of steps. "It has been done, Snowflake. By me. By Mike."

I jam a hand into my knotted hair and pull. "Did either of you fall? I'm just curious."

"Nah..."

"But you weren't drunk," I point out, walking back to him.

"Sure we were. Who'd try this sober? Quit worrying and check out the view." His body arcs over the abyss as he points. "There's the old home place, third trailer to the left of the road. I wonder if that dumb tray Jimmy nailed to the window is still there. Bet no one's put birdseed in it since he kicked." Knees bent, he settles his weight over his heels like he's riding a horse, which is better than the leaning and pointing he was just doing. "Mikey lived next door on the right," he explains. "That's a different trailer, though. His mom remarried and moved away." His weight shifts forward again.

"Get down, Lonny! You look like a jumper."

"You worry too much. At least I know I'm alive. Get up here, Fish. Be alive," he taunts.

"Risk death to prove I'm alive? You see any problem with that logic?" But I have the same knot in my stomach I always get before a big test. To my stomach, flunking a test and dying are the same. Talk about a failure of logic.

He takes a couple of quick steps. "Come on, come on," he urges. "Step right up. Just try it for two seconds."

"Two seconds, huh?" I go back to my safe little life tomorrow and the story will be about how I *almost* walked the bridge rail. It'll go great with that other story about how I *almost* got to first base with Annie Cagney, and the one about how I *almost* beat out Hofstra. Still, I continue to stall. "You know, mentally I'm right with you. Physically I'm only eighteen inches from being there."

"Sorry, Snowflake. Close only counts in horseshoes and hand grenades."

"Horseshoes and hand grenades…? Aw, what the hell." I put a foot on the concrete barrier. "What the hell, right?" The hard edge presses into the arch of my sneaker, and I step up.

The change in altitude may only be eighteen inches, but the nothing below is ocean deep.

"Stay loose," Lonny advises. "Stay loose, stay relaxed. And whatever you do, don't think."

My pulse pounds in my ears but I imitate Lonny. The two of us slouch, rock solid, at the edge of oblivion. And suddenly it comes to me: we are too cool to die.

Or maybe it's that death is not a big deal when you stand right next to it.

"Hey, Lonny." I lift my right foot. "Wanna see me fly?"

A second pair of headlights crests the road on the other side of the bridge and plunges toward us. The driver lays on his horn, and for a second I see what he sees: a kid standing on one foot above a fifty-foot drop, about to pull an Icarus.

I twist my ankle stumbling back to the safety of the road. I can't even breathe. The logic-guy who's been tied up in the back closet of my brain begins to kick his way out. I hang my head over the side of the bridge and barf.

"Aw, gross! You're a sorry excuse for a drunk, you know that, Snowflake?"

The acid burns my throat. "God, Lonny, you've got to get down." I hold out my arms. A sudden downdraft of rain stings my palms and I'm grateful; nobody can be expected to do this in the rain. Lonny has an out now. He'll climb down.

I reach up a hand to him, but he dances away along the narrow edge. "Metal to metal, Fish."

A train whistle cries in the distance. Down the track, a Cyclops eye of light is rushing toward this overpass. The faint *ca-chunk* of metal wheels grows and the whistle blasts.

As the train plunges under the bridge, the concrete reverberates against my feet, as if there's a current passing from the train to the bridge to my body. Lonny must feel it too. "I'm Wile E. Coyote!" he shouts above the roar. "I can run on air!" And he takes off, not watching where he puts his feet, just running.

Safe again on the bridge, I chase him—but Lonny vanishes, camouflaged by the drops that suddenly hit my glasses. "Lonny!" I bawl. "Lon-ny!" But the train drowns my voice.

I hunch over and put a hand on the concrete ledge, using it as a guide. When I catch up I'll knock him back onto the bridge if I have to. My hand scrapes along the edge but I never reach him. The concrete ends. There's a gap of about six inches, then the metal guardrail starts. "Lonny!"

Engage brain, engage brain. If he made it this far—metal to metal—he's okay. But if he made it this far, where the hell is he? The ground angles up from the railroad bed until there isn't any drop-off. If he was close to the end of the bridge rail he could have jumped down, even fallen, without getting hurt. But if that happened, why isn't he stepping back up on the road?

"Lon-ny!"

I jump the short metal rail. My feet hit the wet grass on

the other side and shoot out from under me. As I slither down the grassy embankment on my back, something catches on my glasses, rips them off. I throw an arm over my face, and turn my body just enough so that I begin to roll.

The surface under me becomes hard and steep; I pick up speed. My cheek and nose burn like a struck match—must be on the concrete ramp—can't see clearly—everything blurs. Something stabs me in the side. The clatter of the train gets louder and louder—even without glasses I see the flickering, swaying wall of boxcars, there for a flash, snatched away as I tumble, bigger each time I see it. The gnash of metal on metal swells to a roar—and I'm headed right for it. Slice and dice. Got to think—got to think—got to stop!

I thrust my arms out, bend my knees. Elbows, forearms, knees get smacked and scraped, but I feel myself slow. Then suddenly the ground levels. I flop onto my back in the flat sandy stretch at the foot of the ramp. I lie there, lungs burning. Grit swarms around me. The air tastes metallic. The last car passes. As the *ca-chunk* of the train fades, the rasp of my own breathing takes over. "Lonny?" I can't shout, but even a hoarse whisper sounds loud in the heavy silence.

I roll onto my hands and knees, afraid to stand. Somewhere in this dark—unless he fell on the roof of a boxcar—I'll find Lonny, and I don't want to.

Maybe I should go for help, get someone who's been trained to handle stuff like this. Stuff like what? I force myself to think the words. *Stuff like finding Lonny's dead body.* But Lonny, dead? Not ten minutes ago the man was dancing on the bridge rail, too cool to die. And then I remember

Desiree's dog. Here one second, gone the next.

I have to get to my feet. I have to look for him.

Then, nearby, someone starts clapping. "Damn, Fish! That was beautiful!"

Lonny is a dark blur against the pale glow of the ramp— but even though I can barely see him I can tell he's in his usual easy slouch.

"Beautiful? You nearly get us both killed and that's beautiful?" I struggle to my feet. I want to rip his head off. Without glasses, I hurl my fist at the shape of him—it's like the dying comet move, only without the wasted motion. My fist flies, all my weight behind it—wherever the avenging comet lands it's going to hurt like hell.

At the last second Lonny dodges out of the way. The comet sails past him. I go down, taken out by my own momentum.

"Whoo-ee!" he exclaims as my chin and palms scrape across the sand. "The mouse that roared!" And he busts up, laughing.

I roll, throwing all my weight at him, and hit his legs with my shoulder. I feel his knees give, and he topples.

I scramble up and straddle him, sitting on his chest. "What's so funny?" The stink of liquor rises off him as he laughs. "I said, what's so funny? We're under a bridge in goddamn Ocala. You nearly killed both of us." His sides shake against my thighs. I force his shoulders into the ground. "Admit that was stupid, Lonny! Say it!"

He swats me off, shoving me to one side. I lie panting, flat on my back. "Asshole!" I yell.

Now Lonny straddles and pins me. "Asshole!" he laughs. "Your daddy let you talk like that?"

I knee him in the butt—not a slick move but effective. He falls on me full length with a startled grunt, but I twist out from under him and sit up.

"Damn. What the *hell's* gotten into you?" He sits up too. Facing each other in the dim light, our legs straight out in front of us, I know where he is mostly by the sound of his panting.

"*Me,* gotten into *me?* Look where we are, thanks to you."

"No one held a gun to your head."

"I signed on for two days. You said you were taking me home."

"I was, man, I was. But something came up."

"Yeah, something always does. You screw everyone over: me, your wife, your kid."

Still sitting, he punches me in the gut so fast I don't even see it coming. "Mind your own damn business," he grunts.

"Then take care of your family," I groan, protecting my stomach with both arms. "That's *your* damn business." Still hugging myself, I turn my shoulder toward him and throw my full weight in his direction. I ram him hard.

He falls back, but catches himself with his hands. "Sissy knew going in, I'm not the daddy type."

"Charlie didn't!" I lurch to my feet. "You walked out on him too!"

He's on his feet in an instant. We circle each other. "And you walked out on your father... Nobody's perfect."

"As far as he knows I'm still home!" I shout, taking a step toward him.

"And that makes it better?" He rams me with his chest, sending me skipping back.

"Even if he finds out, I let him down once. *Once.*" When I ram him, he doesn't move an inch. The impact sends a tremor down my body, but my mouth keeps running. "Not you, man. You come and go. You forget to send money. How could you do that to a girl like Sissy?"

His next move is the last thing I'd expect. He reaches out and gently pats my cheek. "Aw, the poor sick puppy's got a crush on Sissy Erle."

I answer with a punch. He grabs my fist, clamps onto my other arm, and jerks me off my feet. When I land, I expel air that has been in my lungs since first grade.

"Mind your own damn business," he repeats, pinning me with a foot planted in the middle of my chest.

I slam his knee back with the heel of my hand, and the pressure on my chest goes away. He lets out a surprised "Damn!" as he falls, but instantly starts battering me with his fists, steady and methodical. Each punch moves me half an inch, cramming sand into the waist of my jeans and down the neck of my shirt.

I lie, curled around my vital organs. Lonny buries his knuckles in my kidney. I can let him beat me until he gets tired—he's a fighter and I'm not—or I can try something. Letting out an ungodly ninja shriek, I uncoil and go completely nuts on him. My flailing arms and legs hit him in the chest and stomach. I figure that the only way to beat him is to be completely random, to never do what he expects.

When he grabs me I throw my weight hard left. We roll over and over. I feel his T-shirt rip as I drag him to his feet, but I jerk him up so fast I fall backward. He's still on his feet, panting. I pop up to my knees. With another ninja scream, I grab his belt and drop him. We roll some more. He's on top most of the time.

"Come on, Fish. This is gettin' old. Ya tired yet?"

"No!" I lie.

He snatches the front of my shirt and hauls me up onto my knees. "Enough of this crap," he says. My feet leave the ground as he lifts me by my shirtfront and tosses me.

I fall—I'm getting used to falling. Only this time a searing pain knifes me in the ribs. I cry out.

"Now what?"

I roll off the railroad tie, panting. "I think you broke my ribs."

"Any of them sticking out funny?"

I run a hand over my ribcage. "No, but they hurt like hell."

"You probably cracked one. No big deal. I cracked three in a scrimmage and went on to throw the winning TD. Just gotta suck it up." The sand makes a crunching sound as he walks away.

"What is it with you, Lonny?" I shout after him. "You have to do everything better. You even get hurt better."

The sound of his footsteps changes. He's climbing the ramp.

"Lonny? Lonny! Come on, man. You have to help me find my glasses. I'm blind without them."

I listen to the scrape of his boots as he continues up the ramp.

"Thanks, Lonny!" I shout. "Thanks for everything."

Each breath hurts, but I crawl up the slick grassy hill, groping along my trajectory. I comb the grass with my fingers. I try to remember exactly when I lost them so I can guess how far down they'll be, but the fall was a jumble. It all went by too fast.

What if I smashed them? Got to stay positive. If just one lens survived I'll be okay.

Rain drips off my nose. The *slap-hiss* of tires on the bridge sounds close. Suddenly I can see the dazzle of the lights on the bridge. I'm at the top of the hill and I haven't found them.

Backing down the hill, I fan my hands out as far as I can reach. For one second I feel the temple of my glasses—saved! What I jerk out of the grass is a wire coat hanger. I hurl it into the dark.

When I reach level sand I climb the ramp back to the ledge and jostle Lonny. "Lonny, if you don't want to have to tie a rope around my waist and lead me you'd better help me find my glasses."

He groans, "In the morning, Fish."

"I can't leave them lying out there all night. Something could happen."

"Damn, I'm getting tired of babysitting you." He bumps my arm with the flashlight. "Here." I take it and go back into the rain alone.

Hugging my ribs with one arm, I swing the light, looking for a glint. All I find are beer bottles.

10

My stomach growls and I open my eyes. My cheek is numb against the concrete ledge. I'm so cold that my fingers barely move. But the worst part is the sun is coming up on the third day—make that the last day. If I don't get home now, it's over. Suddenly, I visualize one of Dad's cards: *It's all about ATTITUDE. Believe in yourself and you can do ANYTHING.*

Believing and attitude aren't going to cut it. Not when I feel a stab of pain each time I inhale. This is scary. The pain didn't go away during the night—I must be really broken.

I have to compartmentalize, get through the day one step at a time, starting with Lonny and me reporting in at Able Body. I push myself up and look around. Without glasses the world is a vague pattern of darks and lights. Those milky splotches must be the security lights over the trailer doors. The sky hangs behind the trailer park like a dirty sheet. It doesn't seem to be raining—but it will.

I smell smoke. "Lonny?" I can just make out the orange glow of a campfire on the sand beside the tracks. The darkish shape next to it's got to be him, hunkered down. "Hey," I shout. "Save a few BTUs for me." He doesn't answer. "Get over it, okay? Yesterday is yesterday." It sounds exactly like something he'd say, but he doesn't answer.

Alternately striding and sliding down the ramp I yell, "Shouldn't we get our butts over to Able Body?" I strangle on the last word; the dark silhouette beside the fire is nothing but an oddly shaped piece of cardboard, too soaked to burn. "Lonny?"

I scrabble back up the ramp, one arm around my ribs. His duffle bag is gone, the flashlight. Everything on the ledge belongs to me. "Damn you, Lonny." In a panic, I stuff my things in my pack and skid back down, but I can't think of what to do next.

My hands are shaking when I hold them over the dwindling fire Lonny built out of cardboard and a couple of wooden pallets. Maybe he got warm, but there's nothing left now but smoke and a few skinny flames.

I have to stay calm, rational, consider all the possibilities. Maybe he went for a walk. Maybe he's somewhere trying to score a pack of cigarettes. Maybe he's off taking a leak. But his stuff is gone. The only rational explanation is this: he ditched me.

What do I do without him? Maybe the plan still holds. First I find the glasses, next I go to Able Body, then I work a day. Finally I walk the money across the street and hand it over to Mr. Avery. There's just one problem with the plan. As the last of the flames go out I wonder if I can do a day's work. I see the scrapes on my knuckles. It's hard to close my hands. I take an experimental deep breath, and the pain in my ribs is so bad I suck air to keep from yelping. *So? Don't take a deep breath.* That's what Lonny would say.

Dad and I call it playing hurt when I go to school sick. What a joke. Right now a sneeze would kill me. *This* is playing hurt. But I have to do it.

Step one: find the glasses. I search the hillside four times, but without my glasses I can't find my glasses. Forget step one.

Step two: Report to work. I check my watch. Crap. The day labor place is about to open. The boss, Mr. Huston, made a big deal out of being on time. I wonder for a second if Lonny's already at the door, waiting to blow my cover, but that's out of my control. For now I have to concentrate on getting there.

I stride up the hill—and that's when I find my glasses. I step on them. They probably weren't in great shape after being ripped off my face and lying in the grass all night, but stepping on them almost finishes them off. When I pick them up they are crumpled like a dead bug. The temples are twisted; one sticks up like an antenna. One lens is cracked and the other is majorly scratched. I can see when I put them on, but do I want to be seen in them? I must look completely psycho.

I wear them until I'm a block from Able Body. Then I set them carefully in the top of my pack.

I arrive two minutes before the door opens, just as it begins to rain. Lonny is there, standing around in the light drizzle with half a dozen other men. He must have bummed a cigarette from one of them because he's smoking. When he sees me he turns away—but not so fast that I don't see the shiner I gave him. What do you know? Geek Man scores.

On the other side of the glass door, looking clean and dry, Mr. Huston turns the deadbolt. We all file inside. I almost cry over the smell of coffee, but it must be in the back room: staff only.

"There's been a change of plans," Mr. Huston says, rocking back on his heels. "We can't paint on account of the rain. The only indoor job I have is hanging Sheetrock."

All I know about Sheetrock is that it's heavy, and right now I can barely lift my own arms. But I have to do it. The pain is on my right side. Maybe I can still lift with my left arm.

"Any of you boys have experience?" he asks.

Three guys raise a finger: one wearing a Land of the Free ball cap, Lonny…and me. Lonny turns toward me like, *what the hell?* I stare him down.

Huston's glance ticks back and forth between us. Last night Lonny told the man I had all kinds of experience. "Can the kid do the job?" he asks.

Lonny shrugs. "He says he can."

Huston makes a quick decision. "I only need two. You…" he says, pointing to the guy with the ball cap. "And you." His finger swings past me and stops on Lonny. "The rest of you boys come back tomorrow."

For a second, the row of Able Body rejects blinks, like babies with the sun in their eyes. "Shit," mutters one guy as he flaps his collar up and steps back into the rain. The others shuffle after him, draining into the street.

I'm still standing there, trying to formulate an argument for why he needs three, not two, and why one of the three should be me, when Huston puts a hand on my shoulder and shoves me toward the door. "Go home, kid. I'm sure your mama's lookin' for you."

By the time I get outside the other five rejects are ambling off in as many directions. They're all a little more stooped than when they had stood outside waiting for the door to open.

Before I start walking, I put on my psycho glasses and take one last look. Through the window I see Lonny bullshitting with the guy in the ball cap, probably angling for one of the Luckys in the man's shirt pocket.

I don't wait to see if he gets it.

He will.

I hug my ribs and put one foot in front of the other, operating my body from a remote command center in some dusty brain closet I've never opened before. The controls are unfamiliar. I can't remember where I put the owner's manual. The dingy-white rubber toes of my sneakers appear and disappear. I have no plan any more. It's Random Walk time. Feet, you're on your own.

My knees feel rigid. *Tink, tink, tink,* my feet move like the points of a compass walking measurements across a page.

I start to hallucinate food. Not great food; I couldn't handle that. I think about the time Dez emptied a box of noodles into a pot of cold water, then brought it to a boil—she said that was how you cook spaghetti. When she dumped the water the noodles were all glued together. She swore that it usually worked and said it would taste fine. Inedible even with sauce, the lump lay on my plate like a dead squid. Now I would eat that dead squid without sauce. With sauce I'd eat the plate.

The rhythm of my feet slows until I realize that I'm not walking anymore. I haven't eaten in a long time and I don't pack a lot of fat. Maybe I've expended my whole fuel supply. If Dez were here this might seem funny. *Hey, Dez, power me up.* She always carries packets of saltines Boots brings home from work. I could inhale thirty or forty packets, easy.

It takes everything I have to raise my head, and there, in a miracle of coincidence, is Desiree's favorite place in the world: a public library.

I want to go inside but when I check out my reflection in a window my hair is doing an Einstein. My sweater's torn and dirty. I stink. And the glasses make me look like a crash test dummy that just hit the windshield at a hundred miles an hour.

For a while I loiter near the door, catching the warm air whenever it opens, but it's like looking at a poster of the Bahamas. It's not making me warm.

Then I remember Desiree's "regulars," the homeless men and women who spend their days at the main branch of the Leon County Public Library. As long as they're not drunk, don't sleep, and don't claim to be the Messiah, the staff lets them stay. Desiree gives them saltines.

Before going inside I try to flatten my hair with my hands but it springs back up. The only thing I can do to normalize my appearance is take off my glasses. I push the door open, hoping someone like Desiree works here.

Without my glasses, I perceive the woman behind the checkout desk as a smeary blob. She doesn't try to stop me, but the light spot that is her face tracks me.

I'm walking away from her when I realize that my feet don't seem to be making it all the way to the floor. The ceiling lights dance. Each one has a glowing aura around it—and they're singing something in high screechy voices, like cartoon chipmunks.

I have to slide a hand along the metal edge of a bookshelf to keep from stumbling. I collapse into the first chair I see. It's a beanbag with a squeaky vinyl cover. A green plastic table in front of it is scattered with board books. The covers are too bright and everything is whirling. I close my eyes in self-defense.

Something nudges my shoulder. "Sir? Are you all right, sir?" I turn away. Whatever it is pokes me again.

"Sir?"

I smell coffee. Am I dead? Is this heaven? My eyes open a slit. Three inches from my nose hovers a steaming Styrofoam cup and behind that a nametag that reads *Evangeline Geissler, Youth Services Librarian* in fuzzy letters.

"Here, drink this. I'm sorry, sir, but sleeping isn't allowed in the library."

"Wasn't sleeping…." I take the cup she holds out.

"I hope you like cream and sugar." She backs away and perches on the edge of the table.

I take a sip. The coffee is creamy and sweet. But between the first and second sips I fall asleep again. My chin hits my chest. Suddenly there's hot liquid in my lap. God—did I pee myself?

"Are you all right?" A hand holding a napkin jabs at my crotch.

"Fine. I'm fine." As my head swings back up, the name on her badge seems familiar. "Geissler. That's like Dr. Seuss's name." I think of Charlie.

"Well, almost." Her caterpillar eyebrows stand up on their tails—the worry position. "Are you in some kind of trouble?"

My shaggy reflection, which looks werewolfish in her glasses, answers, "No, I'm fine. I just need an SAT prep book."

"But you're soaked."

"I'm taking the test Saturday," insists the kid-turned-wolf. "I need a book."

She looks back at me over her shoulder a couple of times, but returns with a Barron's, one that sits on a shelf by my bed at home; I've already done all the tests. "Are you a runaway?" she whispers.

"No. I just need to study. I'm fine. Thanks."

She begins shelving a cart of easy readers, glancing over

at me every three or four books. I open the Barron's and pre-tend to scan a question. Without glasses I can barely read it, but with my glasses I'd freak her out even worse. As soon as Evangeline Geissler goes around the corner with her cart I put my head down on my arms on top of the open book.

"Listen, is there someone you could call?" I wake up with a start. Easy readers shelved, Evangeline is back. "There must be someone who could come get you. Use my cell. I have loads of free minutes." She pushes the tiny silver phone into my dirty hand. "Call your parents," she urges. "Whatever the fight was about, they'll forgive you. Believe me, I know." This is interesting. A librarian with a past. Stockings whispering, she walks over to the desk to give me some privacy.

I stare at the little handset. "Go on," she encourages. Suddenly all I want is to talk to Dad, not to tell him about how he owes me—I just need to hear his voice. I poke the numbers. It rings twice, then an electronic voice cuts in. "The number you have dialed is no longer in service." Click. I stare. The phone is a small animal that just died in my hand.

"That was quick!" Evangeline sings from the desk.

"Nobody there." I cover my face with my hand and try to think. Nana's phone is disconnected. Did Dad finish early and head home? No, this is just Dad being his usual efficient self, getting the phone cut off a day early.

"Try someone else," Evangeline encourages.

So I jab a familiar string of numbers. The phone rings

and rings. Of course she isn't home, but knowing the phone is ringing in her house is weirdly comforting, so I let it ring. If Boots answers I'll tell her what's happening. Unlike Dad, Boots knows what it's like to do something stupid. It's a long shot, but she might help.

Click. "Hello?" The voice sounds hoarse and groggy, but it's not her mother's.

"Dez, it's you. This is so great!"

"Fisher, you asshole!" Desiree croaks. "Where the hell are you?"

"In the children's room at the public library in Ocala."

"Really? Are you really? You never go to libraries unless I make you."

"I was cold."

"What do you mean, cold? Fisher, are you all right? I've been so worried!" She must realize how that sounds—like she cares—because she adds, "I'm used to you bugging me. Why are you in Ocala?"

"I wanted to bug you long distance."

"Very funny. A couple of days ago Holland asked me about you since you haven't been at school. I told her you were with your dad. Which you definitely aren't." Dez pauses, giving me the chance to explain, but I don't. "I know because he called her this morning."

The beanbag chair lets out a rude squeak as I jolt up straight. "He did?"

"When Holland found out you weren't with him she stormed choir practice. She actually accused me of covering for you." There's a long pause, then she says, very softly, "You lied to me, Fisher." For the first time I notice the quiet on her end of the line. No TV, no shouting; I can almost hear her waiting for an answer.

"It just…sort of…happened. You remember that guy, Lonny?"

"That creep across the street from you?"

"Yeah, that creep. He had to help a friend put a roof on her house."

"Her?"

"His ex-wife. He asked if I wanted to go along, I said okay." From behind the desk, Evangeline smiles at me encouragingly, but the silence on Dez's end of the line stretches.

"Why?" she finally asks.

"It was only supposed to last the weekend."

"That's a reason?"

"No. I just wanted to get away."

"Away?" Her voice catches. "Away from what?"

I run my thumbnail down the stitches in the beanbag. They make a little zipper sound. "Dez, look at my life. I study, I worry, I study some more, I worry some more."

"That's you, Fisher."

"But it's not *just* me. It's Dad and me. We're a toxic combination. Dad has these unrelenting expectations—"

"He has big dreams for you, Fisher."

"*His* dreams. But are they mine? I don't know. It's like I'm in a box."

"You're in a box. I'm in a box. Everyone's in a box. And your box is so much bigger than most. In another year you'll be in some great school. I'll still be here…."

"Only if you want to be. You're not responsible for your sister, you know."

She whispers, "Why didn't you take me with you?"

"What?" I change ears. "You, me, and Lonny?"

"You and me—no Lonny. We could have gone somewhere."

I never even thought of it. I went with Lonny because it was easy. "It was kind of a guy thing."

"Like Jack Kerouac?"

"Exactly." Jack Kerouac? Must be some other book I haven't read.

"It's still a lousy excuse. I'm your friend. Not him."

"Sorry." Dez *is* a friend, possibly my best friend, but she's also work. For once in my life I didn't want to have to work.

"Fisher? Holland took me back to her office and called your dad. I had to tell him you were missing."

I tug at a handful of hair. "Oh god, oh god, oh god. How'd he take it?" Evangeline glances over. I fake a smile, then whisper, "What did he say?"

"He asked if you ever mentioned wanting to run away."

"But I didn't run away!"

"Calm down." She pauses to blow her nose. "I told him that if you did run away, you didn't mean to—you do dumb things sometimes."

"Great save, Dez. Thanks."

"Anytime."

"You've got to come get me. I have to beat him home. He won't hit the road until first thing in the morning."

"Are you sure? He was pretty panicked."

"His night vision stinks, plus he has to say goodbye to Nana. Besides, I know Dad. He never does anything spontaneous. Come and get me, Dez. Please? I'll give you my left kidney."

"Boots would never let me take the car!"

"Don't ask. Just come. This is critical!"

"Did I mention I'm sick? After talking to your dad I came home. I have a hundred and two fever."

"Take a couple of aspirin."

"And what about *my* mother? What is she supposed to think when her daughter and her car both disappear?"

"Leave a note. She'll understand."

"She'll be so pissed."

Definitely pissed, and I've seen Boots pissed. It's not pretty. Still, I know how Dez feels about me, and I know that she'll do it for me if I push. I close my eyes. "Forget it. Thanks anyway, Dez."

I'm pulling the phone away from my ear when I hear, "Wait—I'll come."

"But you just said—"

"I'll steal the car and I'll come. Where exactly is Ocala?"

Evangeline unlocks the door of a dumpy Ford Taurus and throws her zip-up lunch bag in the backseat. "Are you going to be warm enough?" she asks.

The sky has finally cleared, but the air is cold. "Yeah, I'll be fine." Arms crossed, I bury my hands in my armpits.

"No you won't," she says. "You're cold already." She gives me a plaid blanket out of her trunk with a few dry leaves stuck to it. "Are you sure your friend is coming?"

"You know that Dr. Seuss book, *Horton Hatches the Egg*?"

"'I meant what I said, and I said what I meant, an elephant's faithful one hundred percent,'" she chants.

"That's Dez: faithful one hundred percent. She'll be here. So...thanks for everything. You saved my life."

She swings the car door open slowly. "Saved your life? What's that, hyperbole?"

"Hyperbole? Who's studying for SATs, you or me?"

"Really, it was no big deal. I shared a few phone minutes I wasn't going to use and split a tuna sandwich with you. Go home, work things out with your dad, and good luck on those SATs."

Before I remember how rank I am, I hug her. It's not like hugging Annie, which felt like the prize you might get for being fifth runner-up. Or like hugging Sissy. That made me so desperate I wanted to absorb her through my skin. It's like hugging a really nice aunt. "So...thanks." I step back and wrap her blanket around my shoulders.

As she drives away she wiggles her fingers at me.

I wave back, then walk to the front of the building to wait for Dez.

For the first hour I count cars, thinking, Dez will be here by the tenth car. When the tenth car passes, I start over; she'll definitely be here by the twentieth car. On my eighth set of twenty I quit counting.

"'I meant what I said...and I said what I meant...'" I rock back and forth, the musty blanket tight around my shoulders. "'An elephant's faithful...one hundred percent.'" It's twilight. The street lamp beside the bench comes on, throwing a circle of light over me. I feel like the Stage Manager in *Our Town*. "Yes, Dez," I say aloud, "I have read *Our Town*."

I'd run up and down in front of the library to get warm if my ribs didn't hurt so bad. What's taking her so long?

"'I meant what I said...and I said what I meant...'" Mom read that book to me every night for weeks. I remember the way she smelled when I leaned against her.

My throat starts to close. For a couple of years after she left, it happened all the time—but it's been a while. The trick is to fill the empty spot with something else. I used to do math problems. Now, barely moving my lips I recite *Horton*.

Horton exorcises Mom, but then I begin to worry about Dez. What if she had an accident? My brain floods with pictures of the car accordioned by a semi or rolled over in a ditch.

Or maybe she pulled into a rest stop and turned the car off and the jiggle-the-wires trick didn't work, and maybe it's one of those scary dark rest stops with the sign that reads "No security attendant after sunset."

And maybe the guy who is about to pull in beside her is a serial killer.

I shouldn't have asked her to come. It's a long drive and

the Vic is unreliable. And frankly, I'm not worth it. I'm only there for her when it's convenient. I'm ashamed of the way she looks. I say things so people don't get the idea that I'm dating her.

I'm still listing the reasons I'm lower than dog shit when I hear the burr of tires on pavement. I look up, afraid to hope. A pair of headlights is poking slowly along the opposite side of the road. One beam shines directly ahead, the other is angled left like Beanzy's wandering eye.

The car, a Crown Vic, rolls past, then jerks to a stop and backs up. It cuts across the center line and pulls up to the curb. The door flies open. "Fisher!"

"Dez! Are you okay?"

"I got *so* lost," she says, climbing out. "I've been everywhere." She stands in the open door, the dome light illuminating her, but without glasses I can't see her features and I really want to.

She comes around the car and I lurch toward her. I'm so cold I sort of topple. As I fall I open my arms, the blanket stretched like bat wings between my hands. I wrap my arms around her.

"You stink, Fisher. You smell like rotten fruit and moldy cheese."

"And locker room. Don't forget locker room."

Her arms hug my chest, hard. "Go easy," I gasp. "Cracked rib." Her grip slacks a little, but not much. "Dez? I'm really sorry about Beanzy." It's a total non sequitur, but she understands. Sometimes it takes me a while to say the right thing.

"Me too," she whispers.

I feel the heat radiate off her as I hold her against my chest. "Hey, you do you have a fever." That's when it hits me; this is the way love feels when someone like Dez loves you—fierce and hard and not always comfortable. It's almost more than I can handle, but I can't pretend it isn't happening. I lean over and rest my cheek on the top of her head. It's not like hugging Sissy; I don't feel desperate. But it's not like hugging my aunt either. There's no perfume cloud; living with a sister and mother who practically bathe in perfume, Dez doesn't wear any. But she smells familiar, like when you walk into your house and even in the dark you know where you are. "Come on, Dez. I'll drive."

"But you're so tired…."

"And you're so sick."

She holds me at arm's length. "Where are your glasses? You can't drive without glasses."

"They're in my pack. I'll drive."

We do paper, scissors, rock. When my paper covers her rock I close my hand over her fist. "Come on, Dez, let's go home."

She laughs when I put on my squashed-bug glasses, then curls up on her side, her head on my thigh. In a few minutes she's asleep under Evangeline's blanket. Between the hot air that pours out the vents on the dash and Dez's feverish heat, I'm warmer than I've been in days. I drive with one hand and hold onto Desiree's braid with the other.

"Wake up, Dez! He got here first." The headlights of the Vic shine on the polished paint job of Dad's Nissan.

She pushes herself up with her arms and blinks. "All the lights are on. It's like he's checking every room," she says. "Want me to come with you?"

"That's okay—you have to face Boots." I open the car door but continue to sit.

"Will I see you on the bus?"

"After three unexcused absences? Yeah, I'll be there."

"See you on Number 47, then."

"Thanks for coming to get me." As I hug her the feverish heat comes through my sweater and, I don't know why, I just kiss her—on the lips. We pull away gasping, like we're trying to breathe under water. I can see the whites of her eyes really well in the light from the street lamp. She shoves me toward the door. "Go on," she says, her voice hoarse. "See you tomorrow."

"Yeah. See ya." I put a foot down on the old home driveway, an astronaut returning from some distant galaxy.

Except for Dad's bag, which lies where he dropped it just inside the door, everything is exactly where it was when I left. It's like no time has passed—and like I've been gone for years.

When I look into the living room, Dad is slumped on the couch, his back to me. Tufts of hair stand up around his bald spot. Dad, always so neat, looks like he's been tossed around in the dryer.

"Dad, I'm home." I make my voice sound normal, like I've been off doing some school-sanctioned activity.

"Fisher!" He staggers to his feet. "Thank God!" He rushes over as if he is going to throw his arms around me; instead they hang at his sides. "Where in heaven's name have you been?"

"I just went for a short trip. You know...a Jack Kerouac kind of thing. I didn't mean to scare you. It was only supposed to last a couple days."

His fingers brush my torn sleeve. "Your glasses...your clothes... Have you been in an accident?"

"No, Dad. A fight."

"A fight!" He almost touches my cheek, but pulls back. "I don't understand."

"You know, two guys punching each other—"

"How did this happen? Who attacked you?"

"I think I started it."

He studies my face, as if he is trying to verify that he knows me. "Where have you been, son?"

"Chiefland...Ocala...around."

His throat constricts as he tries to swallow. "Who talked you into doing such a crazy thing?"

"Dave Traynor's brother, Lonny. You know, the guy from across the street? He was going away for the weekend; I went along. It was no big deal."

He goes white. "Remember Danny Craig?"

"Sure." Danny Craig vanished after hanging out with an older guy he met at a convenience store. They found Danny's shirt in a patch of woods in Wakulla County, never anything else. "But look, Dad." I hold out my arms. "My shirt's right here—and I'm in it. Intact. See?"

"Then you were lucky."

"Give me some credit, Dad! I can look out for myself."

He surveys my muddy sneakers, rank jeans, and matted hair. "Come in the kitchen," he finally says. "I'll heat some soup. You tell me what happened."

I snag a bag of hot dog buns out of the refrigerator and start wolfing them down.

"If you can wait a few minutes…" he says, but I cram in four just to pry the sides of my stomach apart.

I'm starting on a fifth when I look at him stirring the pot on the stove, his back to me. I set the bag of buns down on the table and listen to the spoon scrape. The scene is so familiar. It's the Mom's-gone-for-good scene—only this time I'm the one who'll be doing the explaining. I steady my voice and begin. "This is what happened."

The stirring never stops, but I can tell he's listening. He reacts with a wince or a sharp intake of breath. I hate doing this to him, but I don't spare him. I want it all out there. Things that don't get said may never get said. That doesn't mean they go away.

When I get to Lonny walking on the bridge rail and me joining him, the spoon stops circling. When he turns I see that what little color came back to his face when he realized I was more-or-less okay has drained away. "You almost jumped?"

"Not jumped. More like let go." I wait for him to comment, but he doesn't. Instead, he sets two bowls of soup on the table, thanks the Lord for the soup, and dips his spoon in the bowl. I keep waiting for him to say something, but he just dips his spoon in the soup until the bowl is empty. "Done?" he asks.

I nod, and he picks up both bowls, washes them, and leans them in the dish drainer. He reaches for a towel. This is classic Dad—at the end of the world he'll still make sure the dishes are washed. But this time it gets to me. "Any thoughts, Dad?"

"Is there any chance you'll try 'letting go' again?"

"No, that was a one-shot. I'm over it."

"Good." His eyes get bright, like a squirrel's. "I'm sure it was just the combination of alcohol, bad company, and exhaustion. 'Letting go' is not you, Fisher." He wipes the first bowl with the towel. "Now, we need to think about minimizing the damage. You missed three days. Thank goodness you got back before the fourth one. I don't know if I could have bailed you out—it would have looked like nepotism." He sets the dish in the cupboard. "You didn't miss any tests, did you?"

"You're worried about missed tests?"

"And the SATs. I'm sure you didn't study for them."

I think about sitting in Sissy's kitchen, learning the word for Chinese noodles. "Actually, I did study." Then I realize we're sliding right back into the old routine. I push the chair back and stand. My feet are spread; my weight's over my knees. I'm breathing hard, the same way I did when I faced down Lonny. "Dad, something's missing here! Something is seriously missing! What just happened is *not* okay. I tell you I almost took a dive off a bridge, you say don't do it again and go right back to worrying about SATs." Dad's eyebrows lift. "Don't you see, this is what we do. We pretend the bad stuff doesn't exist. We never talk!"

"Of course we talk. We talk all the time." He turns his back to me and folds the dish towel, then hangs it neatly over the handle on the oven door.

I reach around him, snatch the towel, and throw it on the floor. "You call what we do talking?" My pulse pounds in my ears, as if I've been running. "Every conversation is about *this* test, *that* college application. It's like you're the CEO of some big corporation, only *I'm* the corporation, *me!* You tell me the next move and I stay up all night, cramming. I told you I wanted to let go. But you never asked the crucial next question; let go of what?"

Dad stares at the towel, and I think, I don't know what I'll do if he picks it up. Instead, he slowly lifts his eyes. "What is it, then?"

"The pressure."

"Pressure? I only want you to be the best you can." He's hurt; I'm ready to pull the plug on the conversation when he says, "I never push you—"

"Never push me?" I sputter. "Never push me! Just all the time! Think about it. I'm the only kid who takes his guidance counselor home with him at night—no pressure there. You're more take-home guidance counselor than you are a dad. The only part of me you care about is the straight-A student."

"That's not true! It's just that this is a critical time. I would be remiss if I didn't use my skills to help my own son."

I throw up my hands. "But there are other things, plenty of other things in our lives. We need to discuss them."

Dad sits back down at the table. When I take the seat opposite him, it's like we're in his office with his desk between us. He's in his comfort zone. "All right," he says quietly, folding his hands. "What do you want to talk about?"

"Mom."

Dad squeezes one hand with the other. "What is there to say?"

"What happened? Start there. One day I had a mother—the next day she was gone. Was it my fault, Dad? Did I do something?"

"No! Heavens, no! Why would you think that?"

"Why not? You never gave me an explanation. If you had then maybe, together, we could have done something about it."

"Like what?"

"I don't know. But we should have tried. I still miss her."

"You're not remembering her clearly."

"Yes I am!"

"You remember how moody she was, the way she'd come and go?"

"I know she wasn't the most consistent, she wouldn't win any 'Mom' awards, but you're forgetting too. She did some things great. Remember the Halloween costumes and birthday cakes she used to make? She cared about us. I know you fought, but people who love each other do that. The two of you used to sing a lot. I would lie in bed and listen." Dad lowers his face into his hands. "Then, one day, she's gone, and we don't talk about it? That's crazy, Dad. It's like she never existed."

"It seemed easier." Dad looks like he's shrinking.

"Easier for who?" I tower over him as I lean across the table. "You maybe, not me. I have to know, why did she leave? All I ever got from you was a cryptic analogy about moths and light bulbs. I take it that Mom was the moth, but what was *that* supposed to mean?"

He looks up at me. "It meant that she was always flitting toward something brighter and more exciting."

"More exciting than us."

"Yes, more exciting than us." He lifts his glasses and blots his eyes with his handkerchief. "She loved to paint, you remember." For a moment I can see the indecipherable message she left in blue paint in the bottom desk drawer. "She felt that her talent was more important than family—at least that's the excuse she gave."

"We let her paint!"

"Apparently it wasn't enough," he breathes. After all these years he still doesn't quite understand.

"She sent me that one birthday card, remember? She said she was coming to visit."

"I wish I'd never given it to you. I debated with myself but decided that keeping it from you wouldn't be fair. You were finally doing better, then the card came. You stayed up all night waiting—but she didn't show up. After that you really quit working in school. You acted wild. I thought I was losing you too. I vowed that I'd never let her hurt you like that again."

"Dad...? What did you do?"

He purses his lips a moment, studying the small flecks on the Formica table. "There were other cards and letters. I never gave them to you."

"What?" I thought of all the birthdays and Christmases I might have heard from her and all the letters I never got to write, all the chances I never had to beg her to come home. "Shouldn't you have asked *me* about it?"

"You were eleven. I did what I thought was best."

"You think not knowing has been easy? Where is she now? Or have you lost track?"

"I know where she is," he says softly.

The fortune-teller talked about a river between me and Mom that couldn't be crossed. How could it with Dad locking up the paddles? "Where, Dad? I need to know."

He stares at his own neatly folded hands. "The last I checked she had a small gallery in Lake Tahoe where she sells her paintings and scented candles. She traded us for a gift shop, Fisher." He wants me to hurt the way he hurts; he wants me to take his side. It's the old wishbone play all over again, only Mom isn't here to fight back.

"No, Dad. I don't think so. I don't think that's what she planned."

"Does it matter? It's what she did."

I stare at my own hands, the nails torn up. "She made a mistake, a bad one. But she might have come back if we'd asked her."

He shakes his head. "No, Fisher, she wouldn't have."

"How do you know? How do you really know? Did you even try?"

She might have come back for me.

I stagger downstairs after just four hours of sleep to find a total anomaly: Dad in the kitchen cooking breakfast. "Why are you here, Dad? Shouldn't you be at work?"

"Let them make their own coffee for a change. I'm fixing breakfast for my son."

I pour myself a cup of coffee from the Mr. Coffee on the counter.

He raises his eyebrows but doesn't comment. Instead he waves a spatula. "Have a seat. I'm making pancakes."

When I go to set my cup down at my place, a bundle of letters is waiting.

The return address on the top envelope is Lake Tahoe. It has a Christmas stamp on it. I hold the stack up to my nose, but I guess there are too many miles between here and there, too much time spent hidden in some drawer to smell like her anymore. But her words are inside the envelopes, her explanations. My hand is shaking when I roll the rubber band off the bundle. I flip a couple. Of course they're in chronological order; Dad is such a detail man. I pop the rubber band back on and stuff them in my pack.

"Eat up," he says, setting a plate of pancakes in front of me.

I push the dish away. "Can't. I've got to catch the bus."

He's still holding the spatula. "I thought I'd drive you."

"No, I promised Dez." I stumble toward the door.

All day I take notes with as much commitment as Lonny Traynor devotes to smoking cigarettes, but the information goes from the speaker's mouth to my hand, completely bypassing the brain. From time to time I unzip my pack and just look at the letters. It's not a thick bundle. Not nearly thick enough for five years. Because I never answered she got tired of writing.

At the end of the school day I ask Dez to stay after.

We sit down on a sunny patch of lawn in front of the school. "Here it is," I say, trying to make it sound like a joke. "Time-capsule Mom."

The oldest is a large card. I check the cancellation. "Christmas. The year she left." The glue isn't sticking too well; the flap is loose. I pop it open. "Barney." Mom wrote my old dog's name across the Christmas dog's sweater. "Too bad Barney had been dead for two months by then."

"She didn't know."

I stare at the row of parked cars at the bottom of the hill. "It was kind of her job to know, don't you think?"

Dez hugs her knees.

A crushed flower falls out of the next card, a valentine. The next one spits a ten-dollar bill. She doesn't write much besides "Love, Mom." But what would she have written if, instead of dropping the letters into the black hole, she'd gotten something back from me?

When I finally hit a real letter it's from the year I was in eighth grade. It gives her side of a story I've never heard; why she divorced Dad. I drop the letter in the grass. "So, they're divorced. Nice to know." I lie down on my back and stare up at the sky. "There are only a couple left. I guess she lost interest."

Dez opens the next one. "What?" I ask, picking up on her silence.

"She remarried. Do you want to see a picture?"

I roll away from her and curl up on my side.

Dez fits her smaller body against mine. We lie like spoons in a drawer. I feel her breathing against the back of my neck. The clouds over the parking lot change shape before she says, "There's one letter left."

"We'd better hurry up and open it. I'm sure that whatever is in it makes everything okay."

I don't move, but Dez sits up and leans over me. When I'm looking into her upside down eyes she assures me, "Oh, Fisher, everything is okay."

And because she's right, I can face Mom's nothing letter and her hastily scrawled, "Love you—Mom."

I notice she left off the "I."

"I love you" is too big a commitment for some people.

Saturday morning. "THE BIG DAY!" according to Dad's note on my desk calendar. I have at the top of my agenda the speedy acquisition of some number two pencils. I dig in my desk drawer until I find five, which I sharpen to stiletto points. Like a low-level video game warrior who goes into battle with one kick, the pencils are about all I have. I haven't caught up on sleep. I haven't studied vocabulary since Sissy's kitchen. But I feel strangely calm.

I glance out the window. Today there is no Lonny Traynor lounging by the mailbox, just Dave, shuffling to the end of his driveway to pick up the newspaper. Lonny's brother stands by the paper box and reads the headline through the plastic bag. He walks back to the house looking even more tired.

The road trip is beginning to fade. Relentless study and tests—that's my life again.

I put on my spare pair of glasses. Held together with tape, they look like they go with a costume labeled Geek.

"Morning, Dad."

I set the pencils down on the kitchen table between us and get myself a mug. This is the third morning I've poured myself coffee. Dad still hasn't commented.

"You're taking the SAT?" he asks.

"Yeah."

He looks relieved. "That's next on the go-to-Yale agenda, isn't it?"

"Or wherever, Dad."

"Right. There are plenty of good schools. But you look tired, son. You know you could postpone."

"I'm ready, Dad."

"You didn't have much time to study…"

I smile up at him. "Just my whole life."

He smiles back. "You're right," he agrees. "What's one lost week?" He puts a tentative hand on my shoulder just as I stand up. Because it is unpremeditated, we can do it. We hug like two blind guys who have somehow managed to grope our way to each other.

aleigh rides shotgun. His arm is out the window, his hand air-surfing. "I get community service hours, portal to portal, right?"

"Portal to portal," Dad assures him.

"Because I could work off my time with Habitat and not have to drive anywhere."

Dez, who sits with me in back, her head against my shoulder, doesn't bother to open her eyes. "Your compassion is stunning," she tells him.

"I'll be compassionate *after* I become a hot-shot lawyer. It's on the schedule."

Hofstra sits on the other side of Dez, grinning like a fool, glad to be out of the house under any pretext.

I drum my thumbs on my thighs. "Dad, could you try going the speed limit?" But his eyes in the rearview look nervous. He's focused on the hiss of loose sand beneath the tires. In his mind we're already stuck up to the axles. "It's not too much further," I assure him.

Maybe Lonny will be on the roof. It's been a week and a half since he blew me off at Able Body. If he did what he said, he earned some cash and he's back. If so, we'll help him. But just in case that miracle didn't happen, my ribs are taped. I'm pretty sure I can swing a hammer. And I've brought Raleigh, Hofstra, and Dad for extra muscle—hey, you work with what you've got. This crew will definitely clobber their thumbs—Dez would be better than any of them, but I asked her to hang out with Charlie so Sissy could work on the roof. That way two of us will know what we're doing.

I hang over the front seat. "Turn here, Dad, turn! This is her driveway." The grandfather oak crowns over the scrub palmettos. The roof looms.

"Shit," says Raleigh. "Sorry, Mr. Brown, but you have to be shitting me, Fisher. That roof is way-high, steep too."

"Come on, Raleigh, a 6-12 pitch ain't a ski slope." I say it because I can see that Lonny isn't there to do the honors. He could be in Ocala hanging Sheetrock for Able Body. He could be in Uruguay. Where he isn't is on the roof.

The only one working is Sissy, who stands on the ladder, prying out the nails that hold the tarp to the roof. "Nice butt," says Raleigh.

Dez opens her eyes. "Raleigh, you are such a sleaze!" But a frown flickers across her face as she silently checks out Sissy's butt. At that moment, Sissy turns on the ladder. Her face looks closed. She doesn't recognize the car or the guys in the front seat. She crosses her arms, hugging herself. Charlie, who is holding the bottom of the ladder, turns too.

Even though the car is still rolling, I jump out. "Sissy! Hey, Charlie!"

She shades her eyes with her hand. "Fish!" She scrambles down the ladder and runs toward me, Charlie right behind her. A few feet from me she launches. Her legs wrap around my waist, her arms cling to my neck. Charlie slams into my legs and hangs on, chanting, "Fish is back, Fish is back!" For one moment, this is my family.

Then, behind me I hear car doors open. I turn, staggering a little. "This is my dad, Walt Brown."

Sissy climbs down, blushing to the roots of her hair. "Your son has been such a help to my boy and me," she murmurs, shaking his hand.

"I'm glad to hear it."

"This is my son, Charlie." She nudges Charlie forward.

Charlie squints up at Dad. "He's not sort of bald. He's really, really bald."

Raleigh leans toward Sissy. "Hey. I'm Raleigh." Sissy takes a step away from him and shakes his hand.

Hofstra shuffles his feet. "Greg," he says, ducking his head.

"Nice to meet you, Greg." As Sissy squeezes his hand his ears flame.

Dez climbs out of the car last, a sack of books over her shoulder. "Sissy," I say, putting my arm around Dez's shoulders. "This is Desiree."

Sissy looks from Desiree to me and back again, then gives Dez a quick hug. "Be good to him, honey, he's a keeper."

"Aw…" says Raleigh.

Dez smacks him with the sack.

Charlie is staring at Dez. "What's in the bag?"

"Books," she says.

"Fish can read *Cat in the Hat* without even looking at the book."

"I can read it upside-down," she says.

"For really?"

She drops to a half-squat, her hands on her knees, and looks him in the eye. "Yeah, for really. I bet you're Charlie."

The boy nods.

"You want to hear a story, Charlie?" She holds out a hand.

"Sure," he says, taking it. They walk toward the house, arms swinging. "Say, do you like fossils? Fish does."

"Hey, wait…" I run to catch up with them, digging in my pocket. "I brought you something. It's not as good as the one you gave me, but it's the best I have." I put the biggest shark tooth I ever found in his outstretched palm. "I collected it on Amelia Island."

For sure he notices the broken tip, probably snapped by the dredge that sucks sand out of the mouth of the St. Mary's river to renourish the beach, but he lets it slide. All he says is, "Big one," and pockets it with a grin.

I jump the porch steps and open the door as if this is my place.

"Well, well!" Dad says when he sees one of his own index cards taped to a kitchen cabinet. "'The longest journey begins with a single step.' What journey are you on, Miss Erle?"

"That's a guidance counselor question," I tell her. "You don't have to answer."

But Dad is gazing at her like he really wants to know—which he does—no irony there.

"It's not much of a journey. It's more like a walk around the block. I waitress."

"Is that what you really want to do?" As he gazes at her earnestly, I realize I never asked her that.

She shrugs, embarrassed. Either she doesn't know, or she doesn't want to say.

"Dad? The roof?"

"In a minute, Fisher." He pulls out a chair at the table for Sissy. "You have plenty of options, you know."

She stares at her feet for a moment, then sits. "I never finished high school."

"Not a problem." I leave Dad at the table, preaching the gospel of the GED and community college to Sissy.

Dez and Charlie settle on the sofa. I lead the guys to the stairs. "Follow me."

Raleigh sits on Charlie's windowsill, supervising something he's never personally done. He sees no contradiction. "Lawyers advise; they don't actually *do.*"

I stride down the roof, a hammer swinging in my hand. I place the first strip of shingles and put the shanks of a few roofing nails between my teeth.

"That's an accident waiting to happen," says the lawyer. "You lose your balance and fall off the roof you'll crucify your own tongue!"

I drive in the first nail in three swings. "Not bad," says Raleigh.

The next nail is flush in two. "Wow!" breathes Hofstra.

When it comes to feats of strength, geeks aren't hard to impress. "I could use some help," I tell them.

Hofstra stares at the hammer I put in his hand like he's not sure which end to use. "You can do manual labor," Raleigh assures him. "You're not the pope yet."

"Oh, I'm over that," says Hofstra.

"Really. What's on the agenda now?"

Hofstra raises the hammer over his head. "I'm thinking total world domination!"

"Stellar choice," says Raleigh.

These guys play *way* too many video games. "Come down here and dominate a few nails to start," I tell him.

I wonder if Sissy can hear what's going on. Up here in roof land, it's Fish to the rescue. But it would probably be better if she paid attention to Dad. By now, he's laying out her options, encouraging her to get started. But that's all he can do. After that, it's up to her.

Like Dez says, you choose your wings.

"Hey, Fisher," Raleigh calls from his supervisory position on the windowsill. "What are your plans now that you've torpedoed chemistry?"

"College is still a definite—major unknown. After that, I think I'll join the Peace Corps." I drive the next nail in with a single blow. "I hear that's where smart guys go to do roofs."